LOUISIANA LASS

"Ma'am, a man and a woman just slipped in here. They're dangerous criminals and it's my job to catch them. Did you see them?"

She shook her head. "Out! Out of my shop or I'll call the sheriff. He knows what to do with men who burst into women's dressing rooms!"

"But, ma'am, I'm—"

The full-bodied shopkeeper grabbed a feather duster and pushed it into Spur's face, making him sputter and gag. "Get yer hide out of my store!" she yelled.

Spur sensed rather than heard movement behind him. A heavy object crashed onto his skull before he could whirl to face the danger. He momentarily blacked out, but quickly returned to a hazy consciousness as his cheek hit the slick floorboards.

"Kill him and let's get out of here!" It was a younger, softer woman's voice....

Also in the *Spur* Series:

SPUR #33

LOUISIANA LASS

DIRK FLETCHER

LEISURE BOOKS NEW YORK CITY

A LEISURE BOOK®

February 2006

Published by

Dorchester Publishing Co., Inc.
200 Madison Avenue
New York, NY 10016

ISBN 0-8439-3023-3

The name "Leisure Books" and the stylized "L" with design are trademarks of Dorchester Publishing Co., Inc.

Printed in the United States of America.

Visit us on the web at www.dorchesterpub.com.

LOUISIANA LASS

CHAPTER ONE

Lambert G. Hanover bent his six-foot frame to check his appearance in the mirror. The suit had travelled well. He looked every bit a gentleman, which was what he was counting on.

He heard Teresa's laughter from downstairs where she was distracting the sweet-faced farm woman. It was almost noon, judging from the thin slice of shadow that the sun cast through the window. It was time.

Lambert walked quietly from the guestroom and paced along the hallway. The door stood open, inviting him inside, inviting him to help himself.

The gambler held back a smile as he walked into the woman's bedroom. He wasn't expecting to find riches but most farmers had money stashed away in case of emergencies. If he didn't find anything it wasn't a real problem. They had plenty to live on for some time.

Hanover quickly went through the plain wooden

dresser. Finding nothing, he searched the footed, heavy closet, rifling through tiny drawers of women's underthings, gloves, stockings and handkerchiefs. Again, nothing.

But he felt money in the room. He smelled it.

Lambert Hanover stood in the center of the room beside the quilt-tossed bed. He put his hands on his hips and circled.

An old Bible caught his eye. He went to it and flipped back the leather cover. An envelope fell out. He opened it and pulled out two $100 bills.

He smiled at the money. So the widow's husband had left her some cash. Lambert G. Hanover pocketed the easy earnings, replaced the Bible on the table near the bed and returned the room to its normal appearance.

"Ah, really, Mrs. Johnson, you don't have to—"

Teresa's voice was far louder than usual. A warning. Lambert slipped from the room. Shadows moved up along the staircase. They were coming.

"No, it's nothing at all."

Hanover silently returned to the guestroom, took off his jacket and held it as he walked back into the hall.

"Hello, Mr. Overland!" Betty Johnson said as she reached the landing. "I was just about to show your dear wife some of my things—heirlooms that my late husband brought here from Norway. They're all I have left of him."

"That would be splendid, but I'm afraid that Penelope and I do have to be going. We'd hate to miss that marriage." Hanover smiled at the attractive woman who stood behind Mrs. Johnson on the stairs. "Perhaps upon our return."

"That would be fine! I hope you've enjoyed my hospitality," the vibrant, blonde-haired widow said. "Such as it is."

"More than you know, dear lady. More than you know."

Lambert G. Hanover and Teresa Salvare were back in their buggy within five minutes. As soon as they'd turned onto the rutted road leading south and were some distance from the farmhouse, Teresa grabbed Hanover's right knee.

"Well?" she demanded, excitement puffing her high cheekbones and making her blue eyes glow.

"Well what, dear wife?"

"Stop joking! What did you get? Did the old biddy have anything worthwhile?"

Hanover straightened his back. "How can you doubt me? Reach into my vest pocket. There's a surprise for you, Tessa."

The thirty-year-old woman squealed and pushed her hand inside Lambert's coat. The two bills crackled between her fingers.

"Not much, but it'll do." she tucked the money into the front of her gray striped travelling dress, loding it firmly between her breasts. "I thought that old crow'd never stop talking. Yak yak yak. 'Norway this. Norway that. My dear husband.' I would've tossed my cookies if she'd mentioned him again!"

"I'm glad you approve," Lambert said as the buggy rolled between endless white picket fences. "So why didn't you stop her from coming upstairs? She nearly caught me, Tessa! Besides, I'm sure she had more money salted away up there. You didn't give me enough time!"

She removed her bonnet and flipped a lock of hair from her eyes. "I did warn you, you big oaf!" Teresa patted her chest and shook her head. "That woman was absolutely uncontrollable."

Lambert Hanover shrugged. "That's never been a problem with you before. How many jobs have you done so far? Thirty? Fifty? Not to mention that great week in Kansas City. We should just relax until we get to New Orleans. No more work for a while. Promise?"

Teresa Salvare blinked her big eyes and pouted. "Work? Why whatever do you mean, sir?"

He tightened the reins, urging the horses to move faster. "You know exactly what I mean. I don't want to catch you taking any more women's purses like you did two towns ago. It's too dangerous! Do you have any idea how much we have so far? At least two-hundred-fifty thousand dollars in cash, jewelry and bearer bonds and stocks!"

She flashed her white teeth at him. "Are you saying we should retire? Give all this up?"

"No, no. Not until after we do the big one."

"Good. You had me worried there, Lambert." Teresa readjusted her breasts in the tight confines of her dress and smiled at him. "Although I wouldn't be sorry to stop eating dust for a while."

"All in due time, Tessa. All in due time."

They rode in silence for two hours until the single horse that pulled their buggy balked at going any faster.

"Come on, girl," Lambert said in a soothing voice. "Water and oats up ahead." He eyed the distant spire of a church that showed a town almost hidden in the trees. "You can do it."

The roan whinneyed, tossed her head and plodded on.

"If only you were that manageable," Lambert G.

Hanover said as he glanced at the woman beside him.

"My dear Lamb, you wouldn't like me half as much if I was."

They stopped at a small town minutes later. Hanover rubbed his horse's neck as it drank at a trough.

"I'll be right back," Teresa said as she replaced her bonnet.

"Where are you going?" he asked suspiciously.

"Just you never mind. I'm going to say a prayer in that cute little church across the street."

He guffawed.

"I'll have you know that I was a good Christian before I met you. Not great—just good. I'll be right back."

She snapped shut her purse and strode across the broad street, holding up her skirts and avoiding stepping into the steaming horse droppings.

Lambert shook his head and let the horse nuzzle the bucket of oats he'd purchases at the livery stable. Tessa could be a bit of a bother at times but she'd been a fine partner. With her help he'd been able to more than double his take at every town they'd visited.

But the woman was too volatile, ready to use a pistol or rifle to settle things. Her style clashed with his own smooth, polished manner. Teresa was liable to get them both locked up if she didn't rein in her temper.

Still, she was an asset.

He turned to watch his partner step into the white church. The roan munched and drank, munched and drank.

Five minutes later Teresa walked quickly across

the street.

"I feel so spiritually refreshed," she said, fanning her forehead. "Let's leave now. On to New Orleans!"

"Okay, okay. No hurry."

She grabbed his arm. "Let's go, dear!" Teresa looked back at the church. "Right now!"

Lambert frowned. "Fine."

Ready for the road again after her break, the roan didn't argue as Hanover switched her along Main Street heading south out of town.

"Teresa, you didn't—"

"Come on now, Lambert!" The blonde gasped as she felt the bodice of her dress. "All that money sitting there and no one in sight. Why, what kind of a woman do you think I am?" Teresa said. She dramatially fanned her face. "I guess it must have been a month's collection, or the church building fund or something."

"Did anyone see you?"

"No, silly. I told you, no one was in sight. I sat down and pretended to pray, but that silver dish on the altar filled with money was too tempting to pass up." She reached under her skirts and produced the collection plate. One dollar bill still laid within it. "Those pockets I had sewn into my petticoats sure do come in handy, don't they?" Teresa admired the dish as it shone in the sunlight.

Lambert growled. "Yes. Put that away!"

A breeze caught the dollar bill, sending it fluttering into the air. "Okay. You sound just like my father!" She stuffed the gleaming plate into one of the bags that sat in the buggy behind her, straightened up in the seat and stretched. "It sure will be great to get to New Orleans, won't it?"

"That's a fact," Lambert G. Hanover grinned. He

had to admire the girl's daring. "How much did you get?" Transferring the reins to his left hand, he reached inside the woman's dress.

"Well, ah, ah—don't reach."

Hanover's smile vanished as he pulled a short knife from the woman's bodice. It was still sticky with traces of blood. He threw the weapon into the brush that lined the trail and raised his hand to slap her. "You stupid girl!"

Teresa flinched. "I thought you were a gentleman! I thought you detested violence!"

Lambert controlled his sudden anger and grabbed the reins with both hands.

The thirty-year-old woman lifted her chin. "So I lied. I didn't see the preacher walking up behind me. He surprised me, so I gave him his fondest wish. To see his Lord."

"I don't believe you. Did you really kill him?"

The woman sighed and played with her bonnet. "I don't think so. He was such a girlish man. He darn near fainted when I turned toward him with the knife. I just slashed his arm. He dropped the second the blade touched him. I didn't wait around. I got the hell out of there!"

Lambert G. Hanover shook his head. "What am I going to do with you?" He looked up at the cloud-scattered sky. "You just promised, Tessa. No more jobs!"

"Well, I'm sorry." She tossed her head. "Maybe I have some kind of disease. I'm sure if you were there, and saw all that money just waiting to be taken, lying in plain sight with no one around, you would have turned and walked out without touching it. Right, Lambert?"

"Well, I'd—" Lambert laughed. "I may be a

gentleman, but I'm not that much of one. Okay, Tessa. You're right. You just did what I've trained you to do. But it won't do either of us any good if you keep taking dangerous chances like that. Do you understand?"

Teresa Salvare lifted her pretty shoulders and shrugged. "I guess. Say, can't you make that old nag go any faster? We're still days away from New Orleans and all the riches that are waiting for us there!"

"And on the steamer *Natchez*. That money isn't going anywhere, Tessa. Pass the time like you always do—thinking up ways to spend it."

She sank against him. "That's always fun for a while. And I know exactly what I'm gonna do."

Lambert G. Hanover smiled. "What is it today? Open a saloon? Or a string of fancy women's apparel shops?"

She made a face. "No, that was last week. I'm going to buy myself a ship and sail around the world. London. Paris. Venice. Alexandria—not the one in Louisiana, either. Then on to India and China and—and everywhere!"

"Who's gonna be your captain?"

Teresa smiled. "I don't know. A tall, dark, handsome man who knows how to sail and also knows just what to do to pleasure a lady."

Hanover bit back a laugh. She wasn't a lady, but she sure was pleasant to look at.

CHAPTER TWO

Midnight.

Insects still buzzed in the air. The slow-moving river ten yards to the left slapped at rocks and spoke as fish breached its muddy surface and dove back into their watery homes.

A full moon cast yellow light on the dense growth that fed on the river's nourishment and the frequent squalls that dumped gallons of water onto the area.

Louisiana was muggy, wet and uncomfortable.

Spur McCoy brushed a hungry mosquito from his chin, tilted his Stetson lower on his head and rested the butt of the Spencer Carbine on the log. He hunched forward into a less painful position and stared into the greenery.

Thirty yards ahead the brush quivered in the moonlight. It quited a second later. A woman softly laughed from the hidden clearing. A man cleared his throat. Boots ground against dirt, dead twigs and leaves.

They seemed to be making camp, Spur McCoy thought as he watched the darkened trees. He'd been waiting two weeks to be this close to them, and he didn't intend to let them slip away from him again.

In the darkness before him, the dun horse that had pulled the couple's buggy talked softly to itself. The clanking of the rings and leathers that soon followed made Spur assume that the animal was being unhitched from the front of the rig.

From his position all he could see was the black back of the side spring, two-person buggy. They had driven it so deeply into the heavy brush that the contraption was almost concealed by the lush Louisiana growth.

Spur McCoy didn't like the terrain. The strange trees, the stench of the sluggish river beside him, the silver moss hanging from overhead branches were foreign to him. Where was the high pine country, or the open prairies of the plains states? He knew who he was out there and what was happening. Here, in this wet, rainy state, he was far from home.

Spur held his breath and listened. The faint sounds of people making camp issued from the dense bushes. The crack of the kindling for the fire. The scrape of a coffee pot. The rustle of a blanket.

McCoy fought the urge to rush into the camp. They were probably both armed, he knew, and that made it imperative that he surprise them. He'd been instructed to capture both of the suspects alive. This order put dangerous and difficult parameters on the whole mission. General Halleck's insistence on not killing them hadn't made Spur's day. His boss in Washington hadn't explained in his cryptically encoded telegram, but Spur figured that it had something to do with the fact that one of the fugitives was a woman.

McCoy had worked for the United States Government's Secret Service since its establishment in 1859 by a special act of Congress. It was originally set up to stop counterfeiting and to protect the integrity of American currency. Later, as the only interstate law enforcement agency, its agents took on any type of crime where state borders were crossed. Now McCoy was permanently assigned to investigate any federal law breaking west of the Mississippi.

Light suddenly blushed from the bushes—they'd lit a camp fire. The pair of thieves were having all the comforts of a train.

The telegram had come to him when he was in Denver. A couple of con artists and thieves had swept through Kansas City's best families and left with an estimated $100,000 in cash and at least that much in bearer bonds and corporate stocks which could easily be converted into cash. No one at Secret Service headquarters seemed to know much about the pair.

As he watched, smoke billowed from the camp fire. Spur frowned. It was the first fire they had used in three days on the trail coming down from Shrevesport. They must feel secure being so blantant about their whereabouts.

He'd wait for two hours until they were both in their bedrolls and then rush the campsite to take them while they were sleeping.

It wasn't dramatic or colorful, but all Spur McCoy wanted now after two weeks of tracking

them down was to capture the pair and be off to
a better, more interesting assignment.

He brushed away a biting insect.

And a more comfortable assignment.

His reports had stated that the suspects were a
man and a woman. She was about thirty-years old
from most reports, tall for a woman at 5 feet 8
inches, slender and supposedly beautiful. She had
long blonde hair that she wore in a variety of
fashions. One report said she was an actress who
was good with makeup and disguises. She was from
New York where she was wanted on a theft charge.

The telegram said her name might be Teresa,
though she often used the shorter form Tessa, and
sometimes Penelope. His sources had not known
the last name for her; she usually used her
companion's last name. They travelled as husband
and wife.

The man had been described as an ex-gambler.
Down on his luck, he'd become a con artist and
thief, which he found much more profitable.
Lambert G. Hanover was distinguished looking
with a Van Dyke beard and moustache, fairly short
sideburns and piercing blue eyes. He had dark black
hair, sometimes wore a monocle in his right eye,
and dressed extremely well.

He was at ease in high society. He fit in at lavish
parties and in the homes of the wealthy. It was there
that he did his best work, pretending to be a friend
of a friend and gaining access to exclusive homes,
clubs and parties. The telegram had said that he
was from a poor family from Philadelphia. Mother
and father both deceased. He was a shade under
under six feet tall, strongly built and about 185
pounds.

As Spur recalled the information he'd received about the two people, the campfire behind the brush flared up, lighting the mist that had crept into the air from the river. He heard some low voices and the creak and slap of leather. Were they pulling the harness from the horse? If so, why?

Spur sighed and eased back on the log that he'd chosen to keep his butt out of the damp leaves that littered the ground. He had left his horse back 200 yards and worked up silently on foot. It had been a tough two weeks riding out from Kansas City, trying to find their trail. It was only known that they had left by a one-horse buggy two days before he had arrived.

McCoy had slowly searched until he'd found their trail. It would have been more difficult but the man seemed unable to pass up a promising mark if he smelled a swindle.

So the pair had left signposts behind them as they made their way from Kansas City. One woman in Joplin, Missouri, had complained to the police of being robbed of $50. The description that she gave to Spur matched that off Teresa and Hanover. He'd known that he was following in their wake.

A man in Little Rock, Arkansas, had been bilked out of $300. Another sure indication that the thieves were still heading south.

Now he almost had them. Spur knew it wasn't wise to underestimate the man. Hanover had proved to be an adept woodsman, a smooth talker in town, and a man who seemed to be able to take care of himself and his woman under any conditions.

Until now. Unless something untoward occured, Spur knew that he'd capture them both after they went to sleep. He'd quiet the woman first by gagging and tying her, then go after the man. That would be best. He'd give them two more hours to settle down and be fast asleep.

As he waited, Spur watched the sky. The Big Dipper worked its way around the North Star in its nightly journey. An old cattle drive trailhand had told Spur how to use the Big Dipper constellation as a clock on a clear night.

The two pointer stars on the front of the lip of the dipper cup always pointed directly at the North Star. When they were in the position of nine on a watch, it would be ten P.M. By the time the pointer stars had dropped down until they were coming from the eight on the watch face, it would be midnight. When they lowered to the seven position, it would be two A.M. He pitied the poor city folks who had to rely on their Waterburys to tell the time.

Spur watched the Big Dipper slowly rotate in the sky. The glow from the unseen camp fire died down a little but still seemed to be burning well. It cast flickering shadows on the overhead trees even an hour after he had first noticed it. Were they still awake?

One A.M. Silence from the clearing in the brush ahead of him. But he still waited, wanting to be sure that the man and woman were sound asleep before he walked into their camp. The only sounds he could hear were occasional crackles from the fire. No voices, nothing.

When the pointer stars of the Big Dipper aimed at the North Star from what would be the seven position on a Waterbury clock, Spur drew his Colt .45 six-gun, pulled free the blue neckerchief from around his neck to have handy, and gently moved through the undergrowth toward the pair.

Long training had taught Spur to work through the trees and brush without a sound. Moving like an Indian, he never let a branch or bough snap back after passing. He never put his full weight on his foot for the next step until he was sure there was nothing under it that would make any kind of noise. He was as silent as a snake.

McCoy slowly moved to the back of the buggy, though he could barely see it. He still couldn't get a clear view of the camp site itself. It took him another ten minutes to work along the side of the buggy so that he could see the clearing in the flickering light of the fire.

First he noticed the fire, which had been banked against a foot-thick log that had been pulled into the fire. The log itself burned brightly but all other material had long since been consumed.

To the left he saw the two bedrolls. He silently moved that way. There was no sign of the horse that had dragged the buggy but the harness lay near it shafts. Strange, he thought. Maybe they hadn't tied it properly and the beast had wandered away in search of food.

Completely in the cleared area, Spur moved quickly, the six-gun in his right hand, the kerchief in his left. Which one was the woman's bedroll? The blankets were pulled up around their heads. He chose the smaller of the two and hesitated.

Something was wrong.

Spur bent and swept aside the blanket. It revealed a cleverly compacted mass of brush and dead branches. Angry, he checked the other one.

The couple had slipped away.

CHAPTER THREE

Exploding with fury, Spur McCoy kicked the empty bedrolls at his feet and ran to the buggy. Nothing of value remained. Lambert and Tessa had unharnessed the horse as he'd suspected. They had done it so that they could ride away right from under his nose.

He saw a carpetbag discarded to one side. It contained a torn dress, a ripped book and a newspaper from Kansas City with a front page story about the big swindle at the Kansas City Top Fashion Ball.

Spur spent little time in anger. He checked the area with a torch and soon found where the horse had been ridden away. The prints in the soft ground were deep, indicating that there were two riders and some luggage on board the beast. They wouldn't be able to make good time, but he had no idea of where they were heading. Spur ran past the buggy and thrashed through the brush to where he'd left his horse 200 yards away.

The tall sorrel heard him coming and whinneyed. Spur had been riding the animal for a fortnight and she was a fine mount, one of those sorrels with a reddish-brown body coat and an almost pure white mane and tail.

He stepped into the saddle and rode back to the small camp fire. Dismounting, he lit a larger torch made from a dry tree branch filled with sap and began the slow process of tracking the double-loaded horse, leading his own mount behind him as he moved.

Twenty minutes later the torch sputtered and went out. He couldn't find another branch that was dry enough to light in the damp land near the river. Spur slammed the dead torch onto the ground, mounted up and kept moving.

The trail had angled generally toward some faint lights ahead that he guessed must be back on the main road south. He couldn't be sure that the tracks would end up there, but it was the best bet he had. Perhaps if the couple wasn't there, or hadn't been past, he could still find a bed for the night. Even some soft hay in a barn would be a welcome sight right now.

Secret Service Agent Spur McCoy settled down to walking the horse to the lights.

McCoy was two inches over six feet tall, usually weighed in at an even 200 pounds and had reddish-brown hair that brushed his shirt collar and came low on the sideburns. He had shaved off his moustache a month ago but it was growing into its usual thickness above his upper lip.

He had a solid nose between green eyes. His lips were a little full. McCoy was a crack shot with any hand gun or rifle, had good hands and rode like an Apache. His face and arms were usually burned by the sun and wind, souvenirs from the countless months he spent in the outdoors. His often rough demeanor and quick gun seemed to be out of character for a rich man's son from New York who had a degree from Harvard University in Boston.

Ahead, McCoy saw the lights he'd noticed were from an inn on a country road. A lantern that had been left burning swung before the door. He assumed it was the customary signal that a bed was available for any weary traveller who happened upon the inn at night.

McCoy was about to pull the cord on the bell just outside the main door when a face stared at him through the small window in the panel. The door unlocked and swung open.

A man in his sixties held a kerosene lamp. He wore a nightshirt with a robe over it. His white hair was mussed and frizzled. The innkeeper stared at Spur with bloodshot eyes.

"Gory be!" he said. "You just fixing to go to bed? Damn near time for me to be getting up."

McCoy threw up his hands. "Sorry. Did a young couple in their thirties stop by here a few hours ago, maybe three hours past?"

"They be friends of yours?" the old man asked, squinting out of one eye and closing the other as he cocked his head to one side.

"Not necessarily friends, more like kin. We were supposed to meet here earlier. I got delayed."

The man shrugged. "Yep, they were here. Ate a mess of sausage, cheese and bread, bought my best horse and rode on toward Alexandria."

"Where's that?"

"About fifty miles down the road, then two or so west. Fair to middling wagon road now. Can take a buggy. They were asking about one. Not a chance to get one this side of Alexandria though. Not unless they buy one off somebody on the road, or at a farm along the way. This couple seemed to have enough money to buy whatever they wanted."

"They should have enough cash," Spur said, unconsciously looking over his shoulder. "They stole it. Fact is, I'm a lawman. Looking for them."

The innkeeper laughed. "You mean that pretty little thing? She's a thief?"

"Yep."

"Hell. She could steal my heart, but the guy with her kept her on a close rein."

"I better take that bed and breakfast and get a late start. How much for both me and my nag?"

The old man scratched the stubble on his jaw. "You being a lawman, a dollar for grub for you and your horse, a stall and bed. I'll throw in a pair of sandwiches to take with you tomorrow."

Spur handed the man a greenback and headed for the barn with the sorrel.

"Take the first stall inside," the man yelled after him. "Moonlight should be enough to see by. There's plenty of oats in the bin by the door."

"Thanks!"

When McCoy came back he found the old man sleeping in a chair just inside the door. The innkeeper woke at once and showed him up a flight of wooden steps to a room and shoved a straight backed chair under the knob. He sat on the side of the single bed, blew out the lamp that the man had left and eased onto the straw mattress. Wasn't as good as feathers, he thought as the coarse grass scratched his back, but better than a wet log.

Spur was asleep before he could turn over.

Before noon the next day, Spur had found the trail again. The couple had stayed ten miles farther down the road at a small farm house. The woman who came to the door told McCoy that the couple had been drowsing in the saddle. They said they had been lost in some woods for three hours and were glad to be back on the road to New Orleans. The man and woman had stayed the rest of the night and left only two hours before Spur's arrival. McCoy tipped his hat to the woman and hurried along.

New Orleans! It made sense. That was the perfect destination for Lambert Hanover and Teresa. Lots of old money in that place just waiting to be stolen.

Spur stopped for food at a crossroads store where the man said he had seen the couple less than two hours before. The store owner was about 30, with a hole in his jaw where a tooth had been knocked out. Spur figured he hadn't had a bath in at least a month. His long johns top served as a shirt. His blue jeans looked dirty enough to stand in the corner by themselves. The store owner's right eye was slightly closed, which gave the impression that he was always winking.

"Oh, damn yes, I saw them. Asked directions. Both mounted and looked to be riding a little fast. Best dressed folks hereabouts. They got down for a rest and the lady used our convenience out back."

"I see." Spur nodded. "Is there anything you can tell me about them? How they looked?"

The storeman chuckled. "I don't know about him, but that little filly had the biggest gazongas I ever did see!" He smiled. "I mean big! A man could die of suffocation between those two huge—"

"Sounds like the pair I'm looking for," Spur said, breaking into the man's sentence.

He guffawed. "She's got a pair alright! Hey, you a lawman or something?"

"Does it matter?"

The store owner stiffened. "Not one hell of a lot. Look, you gonna buy anything or you just rustling up free information?"

"I'll buy in a second. Any towns along the road?"

"Yeah. A little place called Wet Prong about ten miles along. Alexandria's near to forty miles from here due southwest. You heading for New Orleans?"

"Probably."

Spur bought half a dozen eggs, a loaf of bread and a slab of bacon. He paid the man 37¢ and got back on the trail as soon as he could.

As he rode, he thought about New Orleans. It would be an easy place for Hanover and Teresa to get lost. There must be 150,000 people in that seaport by now. From there they could book passage to England, France or half the ports in the world. They could even go back to New York in first class luxury.

He remembered from the telegram and the packet of information mailed to him that the woman was originally from the New York City area. And that Lambert G. Hanover was also a gambler.

Spur rode until dark. The sturdy sorrel had recovered her strength but McCoy decided against going on into the small town that glittered before him. It might not even have a hotel.

The Secret Service agent made a camp off the

road in some brush along a stream. He fried up a dozen strips and had a feast of bacon sandwiches with the fresh loaf of bread. He would eat the eggs for breakfast. When his pot of boiling coffee got down to grit and grinds, he threw it out and went to sleep with his head against his saddle.

Just after daylight, McCoy was on the move again. He had demolished all six of the eggs, soaking up the over-easy soft yolks with the sliced bread that he'd warmed to light brown over the coals of his fire.

A half hour into the new day the sorrel took him down the road. Three miles ahead he found the village of Wet Prong. Spur smiled as he saw the words written on a sign over the barber shop. It had to be the oddest name he'd ever heard. Might be best not to ask what it meant or where it had come from.

And as it turned out, Wet Prong did have a hotel. He let his sorrel drink her fill and walked into the two-story building. A $2.50 gold piece loosened the tongue of the hotel man. He was short and squat and owned the Wet Prong Inn. It sported eight rooms and his own apartment.

Torrey wore eyeglasses, had a large mole on the side of his nose and talked out of the corner of his mouth.

"Yeah, now I remember," he said, fingering the gold. "This fancy couple came in just about dark. They had been riding, even with her wearing a fancy skirt. Anyways, they registered as John and Joanna Ford, had supper across the street and went back up to their room. Haven't heard from them this morning."

"They still in their room?" Spur asked. Maybe at

last he was getting lucky.

"You deaf, boy?" Torrey said. "I ain't seen them come down!"

"What room they in?"

"I ain't supposed to say that." He stuffed the gold coin into his pants pocket and crossed his arms.

"I'm a U.S. lawman. You tell me quick or I'll run you into the county seat for obstructing justice. You'll be an old man before you see the outside of a jail cell again!"

Torrey rubbed his pocket. "Okay. Okay! All you had to do was ask! It's room eight. Top of the stairs, to the right, end of the hall."

Spur loosened the strap over his six-gun as it banged against his thigh in its holster. Going up the stairs, he hauled out his weapon and made sure that the hammer rested on the empty cylinder. He cocked the hammer on the landing and moved down the hall, staying to the left side so that the boards wouldn't squeak.

At the end of the hall, he stopped before number eight. The door was closed. He listened. Spur heard nothing from inside the room. He backed to the far side of the hallway, took a big step and slammed his right foot against the door beside the knob.

The door broke free of the lock and slammed inward, hitting the wall beside the hinges. The room was empty.

The window stood open. Light curtains blew around it. Spur charged to the opening and looked out. A blonde-haired woman sat on the sloping roof that extended from the floor of the second story over the porch. She looked at him, yelped and vanished over the side.

McCoy kicked through the window, slipped and

skidded down the rough shingles to the edge. He saw no horses, no riders, no one. He hung his feet over the edge, lifted his six-gun into the air and jumped the eight feet to the hard ground of the alley.

Spur rolled to absorb some of the force of his fall and leaped to his feet. He ran for the street.

A bullet slammed close past him and he saw the gush of gunpowder blue smoke at the far edge of a second alley. He fired once at the area, splintering off some of the wood, and rushed toward the spot.

No one stood beyond the near corner of the building. It housed a ladies' millinery and clothing store. It was the only place with a door. The thieves must have gone inside it.

Spur ran to the store and went inside. A half-dozen racks holding women's clothes, some cabinets and hat racks greeted him. Just as he walked into the store a woman stepped out from behind a rack of dresses. She had a gown over her head and was apparently trying to get it off. He couldn't resist looking at her pretty chemise and white petticoats.

An older woman came from behind the partly undressed female. "Sir! Please leave! This is no place for a gentleman! We're fitting this lady with a new dress and she's—exposed!"

McCoy lowered his six-gun. "Ma'am, a man and a woman just slipped in here. They're dangerous criminals and it's my job to catch them. Did you see them?"

She shook her head. "Out! Out of my shop or I'll call the sheriff. He knows what to do with men who burst into women's dressing rooms!"

"But ma'am, I'm—"

The full-bodied shopkeeper grabbed a feather duster and pushed it into Spur's face, making him sputter and gag. "Get yer hide out of my store!" she yelled.

Spur flung away the dusty weapon. "Did you see a man and a woman race in here just moments ago?"

"Of course not!"

The woman with the dress over her head remained rooted in place. McCoy couldn't see her face, but her chemise did tent forward over what had to be full breasts.

"That does it!" the rotund woman said. "I'm going to get the sheriff." She strode toward the door.

Spur sensed rather than heard movement behind him. A heavy object crashed onto his skull before he could whirl to face the danger. McCoy fell and groaned as his Colt six-gun slid from his hand. He momentarily blacked out but quickly returned to a hazy consciousness as his cheek hit the slick floorboards. He couldn't move.

"Gracious!" The shopkeeper screamed.

"Shut up and stand still!" a man yelled.

"Kill him and let's get out of here!" It was a younger, softer woman's voice.

"No, Tessa. We're not going to kill him. I've never killed a man in my life and I'm damn well not starting now!"

"Get some sense! If you don't finish him off he'll just come after us again, Lamb!"

McCoy blinked his eyes to clear them and gently tilted his head. He saw the woman drop her dress back into place and fasten some buttons. She was blonde and beautiful. In spite of the pain that threatened to split apart his skull, Spur figured he'd never forget Teresa's face.

"He won't come after us anymore. Instead of killing him, I'm going to break his leg. You know how hard it is to ride a horse with your leg in a plaster caste?"

McCoy gathered his strength. He pushed against the floor and futilely lunged toward his distant six-gun. Before he could close his fingers around the weapon something hard and cold banged against his skull again, jolting him into the black of total unconsciousness.

CHAPTER FOUR

As she stood in the Wet Prong dress shop, Teresa Salvare smoothed her dress, fluffed out her long blonde hair and stared at Lambert G. Hanover. He really was weak, she thought. Weaker than any man had the right to be.

"For God's sake, Lambert! Are you serious about not killing him? Just busting this man's leg is crazy. He'll still come after us."

Hanover laughed. "He just might at that, Tessa. Then I guess I better smash both of them. Hand me that footstool and I'll get it done right."

The gunshot from a .45 held firmly in both hands of the female shop owner sounded like a dozen sticks of dynamite as it echoed in the small store. Teresa put both hands to her ears, her face twisted in surprised pain.

"You ain't doing a goddamned thing!"

Lambert slowly turned, putting on his best smooth-talking smile. He looked at the woman who confidently held the six-gun in her hands, the muzzle aimed dead center on his chest. Her grip was sure and firm.

"Don't you try nothing!" the woman said. "I'm warning you, sir!"

"My good woman! Surely you realize that I was only jesting with the man here about breaking his legs."

"Oh sure, Yankee! With him out cold like that? Hell, I wasn't born yesterday! It ain't no joke to club a man in the head twice with a gun butt." She sighed. "Now you move slow like and walk over to the door. Take yer trashy blonde whore with you. You're lucky I ain't calling the sheriff; he'd make dog meat out of your kind."

"Now madam," he began.

"Lamb, we better get going," Teresa said.

"In a minute!" Hanover smoothed his voice. "You really wouldn't shoot me, would you?"

The woman smiled. "You willing to bet yer worthless life to find out? I've shot a .44 since I was ten. Killed more than a hundred rattlers, and I don't mind adding another one to the list. Move or make out your last will and testament!"

"Come now, woman! A wonderful lady like yourself, highborn and bred and—"

The .45 blazed again. The heavy slug tore into the top of Lambert's high crowned hat and ripped it off his head. The con man's hands shot toward the ceiling.

"That's better," the plump woman said. "Mister, I was born smelling gunpowder."

"Okay. Okay! Just don't shoot again!"

Teresa ran to the door and opened it. She disappeared outside and Lambert quickly followed her.

"Come back and you'll get more of my Southern hospitality!" she said, watching until they were out of sight.

"Trouble, Pamela," a balding man yelled as he stormed up to the woman's shop.

"No, Paul. Nothing I can't handle. Get back to your barber shop."

She waved him off, walked back into her store and locked the door. McCoy still sprawled on the floor where he'd fallen, all legs and arms. Pamela Crowley knelt beside him, pushed his Colt .45 into his holster and examined his head with a delicate touch. "Okay, mister, I'll take care of you." She stood with an effort, went into the rear of the store and returned moments later with a wet cloth.

McCoy softly groaned. A good sign, Pamela thought. It meant that he wasn't dead. The cold cloth on his head brought a quick response. Within a few minutes the big man turned onto his back, blinked a dozen times and stared up at her.

"What the . . ."

"Don't talk, mister," she firmly said. "You just rest now. The two you were after are gone."

"Good." Spur McCoy tried to raise his torso to look at his legs. "Are they broken?" He shook his head.

The woman snorted. "No. I wouldn't let them. I've done a bit of shooting in my time. That man seemed scared to death of my .45."

Pain rushed through his body as he tried to sit. Spur strangled back a cry and eased onto the hard floor.

"You won't be chasing that pair for a day or two. I want you to lie right still while I go fetch our doctor." Pamela shook her head as she looked down at him. "At least, he says he's a doctor. Don't have no diploma on the wall, but who'd expect a real doctor to hang up his shingle way out here in Wet Prong."

Spur grinned at the words.

"I don't even want to know what you think about my town's name." She stood and went to the front door. "If any woman comes in wanting a corset fitting, you tell her you'll do the job for me." Pamele Crowley cackled high and long as she hurried out the front door to the street.

Spur McCoy felt for his holster. His six-gun was back in place. The woman must have returned it. At least he could defend himself if the pair of thieves came back. There he had been, enjoying the sight of the half-undressed woman while her partner had slipped up on him from behind. That was damned dumb of him. Never again.

This pair had turned out to be slippier than a freshly caught trout. Spur sighed. He'd better get up and follow them right now. No sense in losing more time. McCoy reached forward and started to sit. A giant gong went off in his skull, pushing him back to the floor. He shook his head to quiet the ringing. That only started the bells clanging even louder.

He knew he wasn't going anywhere for a while.

Spur found the wet cloth beside him and put it back on the top of his head. It somewhat eased the throbbing, pounding pain. Right now would be a good time for a shot of laudanum, he thought. That's what drugs like that were for. But if he got one he'd want another one and then another and he'd be drugged out and in bed for a week. Spur had seen laudanum—that tincture of opium—ruin too many lives to mess with it himself.

Five minutes later he tried to sit again. This time he got almost upright before his eyes blacked out and he slowly eased down onto his back below all the fancy women's dresses.

As he forced himself to rest, all kinds of crazy thoughts jostled around in his brain. Head injuries could be nothing more than a bump. They could be bad too—permanent damage. He'd given them and he'd taken them more than once.

When he heard the front door open Spur hesitated opening his eyes. Was he blind? As the footsteps approached him he snapped open his eyes in a purely defensive reaction. To his relief, he saw a small man with a black case and a frown.

"Good, you're alive. Feared you was all dead and I'd wasted my trip out here."

"Come on, William Sykes!" Pamela said. "It was all of two blocks."

Ignoring her, the doctor knelt. "Head hurt a mite?" he asked. His eyes bugged out like those of a frog.

"All of a sudden I'm feeling much better," Spur smiled.

"You sure as hell don't look too good. Blood on your scalp. Hit twice on the head could be part of the cause of that." He smiled. "You're damned lucky you ain't dead."

Spur suddenly sat up. He wobbled a bit but didn't pass out. "Where did that couple go, the ones who were in here?"

The store owner moved over so that she could see Spur. "Last I saw of them they were heading into Limson's Livery Stable."

"Probably rented a buggy," he said. "Still heading toward New Orleans. That's the way I'll be moving."

"Not right now, young man!" Dr. Sykes said. "You'd better not try it for a day at least. A hit to the head can cause all sorts of problems. You may feel fine now but tomorrow, who knows? Dizziness, blackouts, loss of memory, even unconsciousness. One guy I knew got pistol whipped. He brushed it off, had another beer and walked home. That night he went to sleep and never woke up again."

Spur reached for the doctor's hand. "If I can stand, I can ride. Come on, Doc. Help me up."

"Don't reckon that's a smart idea," Sykes said. He put out a hand.

McCoy gripped it and stood with surprising ease. "See? Nothing to it!"

But his knees shook. A wave seemed to break inside his head. The room tilted as the solid floor-boards beneath his feet buckled. Spur fell against the doctor, clutching at the air.

Spur McCoy lay on a bed. He groaned and opened his eyes. His feet hung over the far end and his tender head crowded the wall behind him. When his vision cleared he saw the small room in more detail—light pink roses stretched along the wallpaper that covered the ceiling as well.

"You finally awake?" a soft voice said beside him.

With what turned out to be some effort, Spur McCoy turned his head to see who had spoken. A young girl with long brown hair and brown eyes smiled at him. She leaned forward and adjusted the blankets beside him. The scooped neckline of her blouse fell open; he caught a glimpse of the tops of two white mounds.

"I'm awake now," he said as he unconsciously licked his lips. The girl's femininity and obvious charms lesened the dull ache in his scalp.

"Good. Mother told me to sit with you until you woke up," the young woman said. "She told me you saved her from a pair of robbers today. Is that true?"

His slight nod made Spur wince.

"How nice of you!"

The indirect light shining through the window illuminated her. She was slender, short like her mother, perhaps about 20. The girl pressed a delicate white hand onto his forehead, still smiling.

"Just checking with the family thermometer to see if you have a temperature."

"I'm not complaining." Her flesh against his felt so good, so healing.

"Not a trace of fever!" She retrieved her hand. "That's good. Doc Sykes said I should run over and tell him if you had a temperature."

He tried to nod again but the pain increased tenfold. Spur gave her a helpless grin.

"You poor dear man! Don't try to talk, or nod or anything! Mother says I chatter enough for at least two people, like a magpie or something. Of course, I've never seen a magpie so I guess I have to take her word for it."

"They don't, ah, look anything like you."

Spur enjoyed the sound of her laughter. "By the way, I'm Jessie. Jessie Crowley."

"Spur McCoy. Where am I, and why am I here?"

Jessie smiled broadly. "You're here behind the

store. This is where Ma and I live. You're here because Doc Sykes said you had to have a day's bed rest before you go riding off again."

"Oh."

The young woman leaned closer to him. "So, how do you like my bed?"

Spur lifted his eyebrows. "This is your bed I'm in?"

She nodded.

"Then I guess I better get up."

Jessie grabbed the blankets from his hand. "Nothing doing! You're stark naked! Besides, Ma would skin me alive if I let you up. Like it or not, Mr. McCoy, I'm your nurse."

McCoy looked under the covers and saw that she was telling the truth. "Okay, little lady. You win. I don't make it a habit to pass up the opportunity to be naked in a woman's bed." He sighed and looked out the window. "You know the hour?"

"Oh, somewhere after three I'd say. The only clock we have is out in the store. I don't hold much with clocks." Jessie held her arms above her head and stretched. The action tightened the white blouse over her breasts.

"That's pretty, the way you stretch," Spur said with admiration. "It's so natural. Like a baby colt just after it wakes up."

Jessie smiled. "Even though you just called me a horse, I'll take that as a compliment."

Spur laughed. The woman lowered her head, her lips trembling.

"Could I—I mean, I know you're wounded, but couldn't I just kiss you once?"

Before he could answer, a speeding slug tore a

hole in the billowing curtains and slammed into a kerosene lamp beside the bedroom door. Fire burst into life as the liquid dripped down the wall.

CHAPTER FIVE

"Shit!"

Spur McCoy's curse mixed with Jessie Crowley's scream as the exploding lamp sent flaming kerosene onto the girl's bedroom wall. She jumped and gave him the room to push himself from the bed.

He forgot that he was stark naked. McCoy's head pounded and his vision blurred as he grabbed a blanket from the bed and slapped the flames licking the rose wallpaper. "Stay down!" he shouted.

"Okay!"

He barely noticed the fact that no more shots were fired as he busily smothered the growing flames. Moving the thick woolen blanket so quickly that it couldn't be lit, Spur quickly contained the fire on the floor.

That left an orange-yellow stream of flames along the wall. He put them out within ten seconds, surveyed the area to make sure everything was extinguished and turned around.

Jessie stood trembling, holding her shoulders, her blonde hair veiling her face. Spur smiled and held up the blanket.

"Sorry. I guess it ruined it."

At his words the young woman caught his gaze, nodded and parted her lips. She looked below his waist. "Someone wants you dead!" she said, putting a hand to her breast. "They really do."

"I thought we'd established that earlier." His skull felt like it was going to explode, so he sat on the edge of the bed, kicking at scarred floorboards. "Oh, hell, I'm sorry, woman. Forgot that I didn't have a stitch on."

"Never mind about that. Nothing I ain't see before." She lifted her gaze from his crotch with an effort. "Aren't you scared?" Jessie asked.

"Naw. Are you?"

"Well, I—I mean, I—" She cautiously peered out the window. "No one's in sight."

"Good. They probably couldn't resist one last pot-shot at me. I'm sure those two are on their way out of town in that damned buggy of theirs. I should follow them but. . . ." He rubbed the back of his head and shook it to clear away a few stubborn cobwebs.

Jessie faced him and writhed as she stood on the floor. "Why Spur, I don't know what's coming over me! That fire lit more than the wallpaper!"

"Hmmmm?"

Delicate white hands travelled up and down the woman's torso and thighs. "I'm all excited. The danger! The blazing inferno! It's—it's—oh, Spur!"

Spur grinned as the woman panted before him, writhing like a cat.

"You want to do something about it?"

"Sure!"

"What about your mother?"

"It's no problem. She closed up the store early and went to fit Mabel Ledet for a wedding dress. Said she'll be there until all hours. And it's two miles south of town." Jessie turned around and bent to close the window. She shut what was left of the curtains.

The movement stretched her tight skirt, revealing the luscious rounds of her bottom. Spur stared at it, at her, and eased his naked body full length onto the bed.

"Come here!" he barked.

She caught her breath and turned to him. "What?"

"I said, come here! My brain's the only thing not working right now!"

Jessie Crowley fell onto the mattress beside him. Their bodies banged together. Spur enjoyed the softness of the woman. He took her head in his hands.

"Ma told me to get you something to eat. I should be going to the kitchen." She slowly blinked.

"You'll do just fine." He pushed his face between her breasts, nuzzling the fabric that vainly tried to cover the gap between them.

Jessie moaned softly and pushed him away. "Here. Supper's already ready." She opened the buttons on her white blouse, frantically ripping them until the garment fell from her shoulders, revealing her bare, upthrust breasts.

Spur sighed at the pink tips of her areolas. "Nothing I like better than Southern cookin'."

He took them in his hands and kissed Jessie's nipples. The young woman gasped at the contact of

his wet mouth and tongue on her sensitive flesh. He
sucked and gently teethed her.

"Mmmmm. I love a man who likes to eat and
doesn't mind showing it!" she said.

"I could eat all day," he said as he switched from
one soft mound to the other.

"But we better not let Ma find us like this. Just
a moment, Love."

She sprang from the bed and lodged the top of
a straight-backed chair under the doorknob. Spur
smiled at the bounce of her breasts as she skipped
back to the bed. "Now, where were we? Oh yes!"

A cool hand ruffled the fur on Spur's chest. His
whole body tingled as her hand teasingly moved
lower, hesitated at his navel, then scraped his
thicker pubic hairs. The nearness of her fingers
drove him crazy. Bloody poured to his groin to
display his obvious arousal.

"You hungry too?" McCoy asked.

Jessie Crowley firmly gripped his hardening
penis. "Famished! Absolutely starved!" The young
woman slapped her tongue against Spur's organ
and licked. "Mmmm."

Despite the dull throb in his skull, Spur knew he
couldn't take much more of that. She tasted his
spasming penis and took his testicles in her hand.

"Hey, little woman! Get on up here!"

"Why, sir, I'm just getting started!"

But she bent toward his face. As they kissed,
trading tongues in a lashing, liquid exchange, Jessie
grabbed his head. McCoy groaned and broke off
the kiss.

"Oh! I'm sorry, Spur! I forgot!"

"It's okay."

Jessie lowered her brows. "Look, honey. Maybe

I better do all the work."

"I won't argue with you. But don't you think you're overdressed for this party?"

"Hmm? Oh, of course!" The woman slithered out of her skirt, and chemise and petticoats, flinging the feminine clothes onto the floor. "There! That's much better!"

Their bare bodies molded together. Jessie's fingernails scraped along Spur's biceps as they clenched. Another kiss. He thrust his groin against the woman on top of him. His passion grew.

She unsealed their lips and huffed. "Okay, lover boy. Just lie back and enjoy it!"

Jessie moved her hips over his crotch. Reaching down between her legs, she gripped the base of his erection and pointed it straight up. A quick repositioning was all that was necessary. She lowered her body, caught his hardness and sank onto it.

Spur kicked as their bodies connected. The angle was perfect and so was the woman. She hit home, rose and bucked, pushing her hips up and down and back and forth. Her moans and the sweet sensations made every nerve in Spur's frame burn.

"Oh yes!" Jessie said, obviously enjoying herself. Her juices lubricated them both, allowing the young woman to more fully impale herself. Her bottom slapped against his thighs.

Spur stared at the lovely face, at her breasts jogging before her, at the woman's unashamed expression of pure delight. He took her waist in his hands. Jessie's knees sank onto the bed on either side of him. She lifted up on her hands and rode him like a bucking bronco surging into an all-out gallop.

Heated flesh slapped together. The scent of her

perfume permeated the room. Spur thrust up into
her, meeting her downward strokes, increasing her
pleasure and his.

"Yes. Yes!" Jessie gasped. She stared at him for
as long as she could, arched her back and yelled as
pure sensation exploded through her beautiful
body.

She continued to bang onto his erection as she
rolled through her climax, heightening Spur's
pleasure. Tears squeezed from the panting woman's
eyes. She shook like an aspen in the wind, flinging
her head back and forth, gasping and shrieking.

Spur McCoy felt the familiar tightening in his
scrotum. He gritted his teeth and pushed harder
into her. His hips came alive, spastically jabbing,
thrusting, driving into her body.

"God. God!"

Jessie trembled through another orgasm. Her
contractions around him pushed Spur over the
edge. He went blind and roared as their pelvic bones
crashed together, as he pumped out his seed into
her willing body, as the woman fell onto him and
clutched his sweating shoulders and rode him
harder, milking him of every drop until he was a
senseless mass of flesh on the soaked bedsheets.

In the timeless moments that followed, Spur felt
Jessie's breath against his mouth. He pecked her
lips but there didn't seem to be enough air in the
room. Gasping, feeling the thousand explosions that
had raged through him finally taper off, he pressed
his cheek to hers and held the young woman until
the room brightened and he had recovered.

Spur tried to speak but all he could produce were
grunts and guttural words. He laughed and licked
her neck.

"Mmmmmm," was all she could say.

A half hour later, when the sweat on his body had cooled to a chilling sheen, Spur felt the girl stirring on top of him. He removed his arms from her neck as Jessie pushed onto her hands and looked down at him.

"I do declare!" she said.

"You, ah, declare what?"

The blonde beauty smiled. "My late daddy said learning to ride a horse would never do me any good. He sure was wrong!"

Spur laughed.

"Oh heck! It's way past supper time. We better get some real food."

"Whatever you say, Jessie. I never argue with a woman who's still got me inside her."

"Spur McCoy, you nasty boy!"

She playfully slapped his shoulder and slipped off his softening penis. "I'll go see what I can find in the kitchen. Don't you run away now!"

"Yes ma'am."

Jessie grinned as she got up from the bed, removed the chair from under the door and disappeared into the hall.

He laced his fingers behind his head, carefully avoiding the damaged areas, and stared at the ceiling with a relaxed smile. He wasn't even going to think about Teresa and Hanover until tomorrow. They were in a buggy. It would be easy to track and they'd have to stick to the roads. Sure, tomorrow was soon enough to think about work.

Jessie rushed into the room carrying a basket. It pressed her breasts almost flat, but they quickly recovered their normal shapes as she set the box on the edge of the bed. Her eyes glistened with delight.

"Guess what I found?" she asked him.

"Ah, a foot-long sausage?"

She laughed. "No, that was before! I found some sliced ham. I didn't know we had it." She removed the top of the basket. "I also have some bread, mustard, horse radish and two bottles of beer. Also some brandy." She poked through the basket. "There are some peaches picked just two days ago—fresh and almost busting out with juice. And a big slab of cheese. Think that's enough?"

Spur licked his lips and rubbed his hands together. "For starters," he said. "You really worked up my appetite, little lady."

Jessie glanced at his crotch. "Me too." She pushed the basket toward the foot of the bed and kissed Spur's bristly cheek.

"What's that for?" he asked, staring at her.

"For coming into my life—even with a lump on your head. For giving a bored country girl a little fun!"

"You're welcome, but the pleasure was all mine. What about supper?"

Jessie laughed. "Who the hell cares about food?" The blonde woman kicked the basket onto the floor.

"Hey!" Spur protested. "There goes our supper!"

"Correction—*your* supper. I got what I wanna eat right here." She gripped his shrunken shaft.

"Now, Jessie!" Spur began. "I can't guarantee—ah—um—hell! How do you know I'm not too hungry to—ah—well—to go again so soon?"

"Why Spur McCoy!" She manipulated him, rubbing up and down with a delicately firm hand. "It would be against my Christian morals to force you into doing anything you don't want to do!" Jessie stroked harder.

He laughed. "It wouldn't exactly be force." He felt a tightening between his legs. "Uhhnh! Little lady, you do that good!"

"Do I?" She turned innocent eyes to him.

"Yes."

"Think you can put off supper for a while? Say, an hour or two?"

"I surely do." He grinned and leaned back. "You're pretty convincing, gal." Spur's mouth hung open as the young woman stroked him.

Within seconds she wrapped her fingers around his full-blown erection and smacked her lips. "What have we here?"

"You know darn well what that is!" Spur said as his left leg involuntarily flexed at the new surge of sexual arousal flowing through his body.

"Are you responsible for this?" She pressed his penis between her soft breasts and grinned as she saw it was too long to completely bury.

"No. You are."

"Oh. Should I kiss it?" She pulled back from him and turned her questioning eyes toward Spur's.

"If you want. I promise it won't bite you."

Jessie smiled, held her mouth over the engorged head and let out her breath. The warm air made Spur tingle and grab the sheets in exquisite pain.

"That ain't fair, girl! Teasing a wounded man like that! I'm going out of my head!"

"Not this one." She moved her hand to its base and slid his penis between her lips.

As the woman vigorously worked him over, as Spur propped his head on a pillow to watch, as he gently took her ears in his hands and guided her movements, McCoy knew why they called the small Louisiana town Wet Prong.

CHAPTER SIX

Spur rubbed the back of his head. Jessie had carefully washed the dried blood from his wounds last night before they'd gone to sleep. She'd also rubbed some ill-smelling herbal ointment onto them. His fingers discovered that the area was still tender. But in the ten minutes or so since he'd dragged himself from bed he'd noticed no dizziness or delayed side effects.

The Secret Service agent stepped over the shattered remains of the gunshot kerosene lamp in the darkened room. Outside, a few birds opened their throats. It was almost dawn.

As he put on his Stetson, Spur heard the girl whisper in her sleep. Jessie Crowley was a fine young woman, but he didn't want to give her any chance of talking him out of leaving immediately.

Fully dressed, he smiled at Jessie, blew her a kiss and walked out the door. Labored breathing told him where her mother had installed herself. He tiptoed past the door but it quickly opened.

"Mr. McCoy!"

He turned and smiled. Soft light spilled from Pamela Crowley's bedroom. "Mrs. Crowley." Spur removed his hat.

The middle-aged woman pulled a nightgown around her plump form. "You feeling well enough to go out travelling this morning?"

"I sure do."

"At least let me make you some breakfast." She brought a candle from her bedroom and started walking toward him down the hall. The dancing flame illuminated her soft, kind face.

Spur backed. "Thank you, no. I have to get back to my assignment. You've been a great help. Thanks for—"

"Oh, shush about that! I couldn't stand back and watch that man break your legs—or that hellion shoot you! After all, I'm a human being."

"I'm greatly obliged."

"Did my daughter take good care of you?" Pamela Crowley asked, beaming at him.

"Yes. She's a wonderful doctor. Ah, good morning, Mrs. Crowley."

"Good morning, Mr. McCoy."

He hurried from the house.

The morning air was unusually crisp. Fog hung over the streets and blotted out the two-story buildings on distant blocks. It smelled of dampness and rain and rotting vegetation. Spur replaced his Stetson and ampled down the uneven, dark street. His head felt fine. His legs worked well.

He was okay.

The sorrel he'd rented was still at the hitching post behind the hotel where he'd left it. She hadn't been

fed or watered. The mare snorted, shook her head
and danced. Spur rubbed her head and walked the
beast to the livery stable. A weary-eye man, just ris-
ing to go to work, accepted McCoy's money and let
him help himself to all the water and oats that the
horse could take.

Fifteen minutes later she was ready to be off. So
was he. As he stepped into the saddle, Spur did a
mental check. His canteen was full, though water
was never a problem in this rain-soaked country.
He didn't have any food, but there should be plenty
of places to grab some grub.

It was time to be moving on.

"Come on, old girl!"

Spur slapped the horses' flanks with his heels.
The slight pressure was enough to send her
charging south along Moss Avenue. To his left, Spur
saw the sky lighten to a dull blue behind the
towering trees. A new day, a new urgency to find
Lambert G. Hanover and Teresa. He quickly left
Wet Prong behind him, guiding his horse on the
empty road.

They must still be heading for New Orleans. As
the sun rose in the east Spur could finally see the
trail. There were dozens of buggy tracks just
outside of town, but as he continued to ride most of
them turned down country lanes. Soon only one set
moved down the old wagon road.

After ten minutes Spur stopped, stepped down
and looked at the tracks. There didn't seem to be
any sign of broken treads or loose wheels—nothing
to help him identify them at a later time. He'd have
to reply on his instincts.

McCoy lifted into the saddle and galloped the
sorrel for half a mile more, eased off and let her

follow the tracks at a walk. Because Lambert and
his lady had left early yesterday afternoon, they
would have been well ahead of him before they'd
stopped to rest last night.

Knowing something of their background, Spur
figured they'd likely choose a farmhouse or a
country inn. The pair probably wouldn't be doing
any more camping, he thought with a wry grin.

The trail continued due southeast along the
wagon road. Here and there, farm wagons had
obliterated the buggy tracks, but the same thin
wheel marks always showed themselves again
further along the road.

Two hours after dawn Spur let the sorrel rest and
take a drink. He rubbed her down and surveyed the
plant-rich land. Birds flew in unison overhead. A
rabbit hopped by without a care for its safety. A
thick-bodied snake slithered through the plaintains
and coneflowers that dotted the ground near the
stream.

Then he heard it. The unmistakable sound of a
buggy approaching. The road went around a bend
50 yards from him so he heard it well before he
saw it.

Spur drew his Colt and waited.

A minute later he holstered his weapon. It was
a strange sight. Two Catholic nuns, dressed in black
and white habits, waved at him as their broken-
down buggy rattled behind their broken-down nag.
He returned their greeting and got a good look at
them as they passed by. Both must have been at
least sixty.

"Come on, girl; let's do it."

The horse whinneyed.

By four o'clock he approached a farm house near

the road. The buggy tracks he'd been following had been wiped out again by farm traffic. Spur turned in at the house and reined up at the back door, knowing that only ministers and salesmen use the front door of a farm house.

He knocked. A worn woman in her thirties walked into sight, wiping her hands on a large blue apron. Her hair had been tied into a bun at the back of her neck. A three year-old boy ran for her and hugged his mother's leg.

"Afternoon, ma'am," Spur said, touching the brim of his hat.

"Menfolk are inside," she said, looking past him and noticing his holster. "What you want?"

Spur knew that the menfolk were out in the fields. She was alone and scared.

"Not wanting to bother you, ma'am, but I was wondering if a couple in a buggy stopped by here last night, wanting a place to sleep. She's rather tall and blonde. He's tall too with dark hair."

The woman nodded and even managed a smile. "They did indeed, sir! Said they was from New Orleans and was rushing back there. Paid me two dollars for a room and supper and breakfast. Land sakes, I ain't seen two dollars in two years!"

Spur nodded. "I suppose they left this morning, right?"

"Fact is, they did. Said they were going to Alexandria, then on to New Orleans." She smiled. "I haven't been there since my son ran off with—well, you probably don't want to hear about all that."

"I'll be moving on. You, ah, haven't noticed anything missing around your place, have you?"

"Missing?" She thought. "A sow ran off in the night a week back. That's about all. Why?"

"I'm a lawman. Both of those people are wanted. They're smooth-talking thieves. Con artists."

The farm woman knitted her brows. "Land sakes. They seemed so nice!"

"Yes, ma'am. That's their job." He reached into his pocket and sniffed the air. "Am I mistaken or is that peach pie I smell cooking?"

"Yes it is. Would—would you like to stay for a slice? I've got two of them bubbling in the oven right now. There'll be plenty for everyone."

"It's tempting, but no thanks." Spur held out his hand. "I appreciate your help, ma'am."

"Why, it isn't no trouble talking to a lawman!" She took his hand.

McCoy slipped her a silver dollar and turned before the woman could protest.

"Well, thank you, sir! Thank you so much! Lord, this is a fine day!"

He smiled as he mounted up and headed south on the road. Spur soon spotted the buggy tracks again. At least Lambert and Teresa hadn't changed their plans—or route. They'd probably figured that he'd given up and left them alone.

But then again, they didn't know Spur McCoy.

An hour later, still two hours before sunset, he rode into a thick forest. Huge, ancient trees bent over the wagon road from both sides. Their branches met overhead, plunging the area into flickering shadows. Yard-long strands of Spanish moss brushed Spur's Stetson. His sorrel balked and sniffed the air as they trotted into the secluded portion of the buggy road.

"Steady, girl," Spur said. "What's the matter? Smell something?"

As he rode, letting his protesting horse pick its

way as slowly as it wanted, McCoy tried to form images in his mind of Lambert G. Hanover and his lovely lady, Teresa. She should be easy to remember, but as he tried to recall her face he came up with a blank. All he could dredge from his mind was a dazzling image of a woman—blonde, tall, but no details.

Hanover's face was even murkier. Spur removed his hat and rubbed the bumps on his head. Maybe those blows had done more damage than he'd suspected.

But he remembered that he'd been reeling when he saw the con artists. His head had been aching, his vision wasn't perfectly clear. Would he recognize them again if he met them on the street, away from their buggy?

Putting on his hat, McCoy didn't know. To make matters worse, the woman was supposed to be expert at changing her appearance, mannerisms and forms of speech. An ex-actress from New York.

"Come on, girl, let's get a move on!" he said to the mare. He didn't want them to reach New Orleans. If they landed there before he caught them, they could blend right into the masses of people and drop out of sight forever.

The sorrel slowed its pace and finally stood still, despite Spur's urgent words and signals. It had decided it was time to stop. Frustrated at this new and irritating behavior, he dismounted. The horse wandered through the underbrush in search of the river that trickled beside the wagon road.

He wiped his forehead. The humidity had stuck his clothing to his body. Dragonflies droned and jerked to and from the shafts of light that penetrated the overhead leaves and branches.

Spur McCoy went to the side of the road, leaned against a tree and watched as a large spider casually walked right up its roughly barked trunk.

The slop-slop of the horse's drinking lulled him. Spur shook his head and yawned. He had to go. No time to waste.

"Come on, girl!" he called sharply.

The sorrel whinneyed.

"Now! Get over here!"

To his surprise, the horse pranced up to him, its eyes shining and the breath blasting from its huge nostrils.

Spur smiled. "You had me worried there for a minute," he said, and rubbed the beast's neck.

Something hit his shoulder as he stepped into the saddle. Spur looked up but quickly ducked as pebbles and rocks rained onto him from the towering trees above.

"Damn it!"

The sorrel went crazy. A stone hit Spur's head. He groaned and slumped in his saddle.

CHAPTER SEVEN

Spur McCoy regained consciousness just as he started to slip off his horse onto the ground. The stones that had fallen from the trees halted. In a moment of blinding pain, augmented by his sorrel's jostling, frenzied kicking, McCoy shook his head and looked up at the old pecan trees.

"Jesus Christ!" he said, trotting the horse in circles. "Who the hell's up there?" His head ached, pounded. Spur removed his Stetson and rubbed his bumpy scalp. Fortunately, he couldn't feel any fresh blood oozing from the wounds but he was still dizzy.

High-pitched laughter echoed from the trees.

But he could still talk. "Show yourselves," he said, swaying on the saddle before righting his body. *"Now!"*

The chuckles halted.

"I mean it! You've got ten seconds. If I don't see you I'll fire into the trees and hope I get lucky!" McCoy drew his Colt .45 six-gun and waved it above his head. Two densely foliaged pecans rustled and fell silent.

"Five seconds!"

Nothing happened.

"Four . . . three . . . two . . ."

A pair of dirty-faced boys dropped directly onto the dirt before him from the trees, rolled in the dust and sprang to their feet.

Spur smiled at the unexpected sight. They're just kids, he thought. Dirty-faced, rambunctious children. He holstered his weapon.

"Whaddya doin' here, Yankee?" a brown-haired lad asked as he rubbed his running nose.

His pal threw an arm around the other boy's shoulders. He was pudgy and dressed only in a ragged pair of denims. "We don't like your kind! Ain't that right, Lucius?"

Spur fought off a smile. "What does it look like? I'm travelling. That's what roads are for."

"Sure!" Lucius grabbed his mud-caked suspenders and turned to look at his friend. "He wuz spying on us, Matt. Just like I thought. Lookin' around for some innocent Southern boys so he could kidnap them." His eyes lit up. "Think that Yankee's gonna torture us now?"

Spur growled at them.

"Yeah. He looks mean enough."

"Shut your mouths, boys!" McCoy said. He rubbed the top of his head. One well-aimed rock had increased the pain in his old injuries.

They stuck out their tongues and pushed their thumbs into their ears.

He stifled a laugh. "You boys do this often?" McCoy said in a stern voice. "You could kill someone, throwing rocks onto their heads!"

"We don't care! We're just protecting ourselves!" Lucius said, shaking his head back and forth and wiggling his fingers.

"Against what?"

"Wicked Yankees who're coming to steal all our land!" Matt said.

"Boys, that was years ago. During and after the war between the states. That's been over for, oh, five or six years at least. No one's fighting any more."

"Still 'an all . . . ." Lucius said.

Spur smiled at them, tipped his hat and turned the sorrel south. "Ask your father if the war's still on. He'll set you straight."

Matt laughed. "Heck, Pa's the one who put us up in them there trees to watch the road!" He stepped closer to Spur. "If I yell my head off he'll come down here and shoot you until you're dead."

McCoy shrugged and kicked his mount's flanks. "Go!" he said in a strong voice.

The horse gladly followed the command. As he rode away McCoy turned back. The boys scooped up the rocks they'd just thrown and hurled them after him. He was soon out of range.

Just what he needed, he thought as the trees separated overhead and the late afternoon sunlight spilled onto him again. A pair of ragged Southern defenders.

Teresa Salvare frowned as they stood on the banks of the Mississippi River next to their buggy. "What a backwater town!" she said staring at Baton Rouge. A hot breeze ruffled the woman's pink bonnet. "Lamb, there's nothing to see here. How much longer until we get to New Orleans? Honestly,

I can smell all that money downstream!"

Lambert G. Hanover spread out his hands. "Patience, Tessa. Baton Rouge has many fine houses. Sure, it isn't New Orleans, but it's a rich field for our business."

Teresa tapped her booted foot. "I don't care. Let's get back on the road."

He turned to her. "We still have a few days until the race begins. Why shouldn't we do some business here? It won't take more than two days to get to New Orleans. We have plenty of time, my dear."

Teresa crossed her slender arms. "Lambert, we're going. I can't stand this place!"

"This isn't like you, Tessa. My good woman, you robbed a country church of its collection yesterday! Are you getting highbrow on me?"

She smiled and took his arm. "No. Just more selective. Come on!"

The thirty-year-old woman dragged Hanover to the buggy. He sighed and climbed onto the seat.

"Maybe you're right," he said as Tessa settled down beside him. "No sense in taking needless risks way up here when everything we've been waiting for is so close. Alright, my dear. We'll go."

Teresa threw back her head, took off her bonnet and ruffled her blonde hair. "Lamb, I still wish we were going to board the *Robert E. Lee*. The *Natchez* just isn't as good a sternwheeler."

He smirked at her. "When did you become expert in these matters?"

The woman affected a broad Southern accent. "Why suh, I was bohn and raised in New'ahlins! You know that!"

"You know why we have to take the *Natchez*," Hanover said, ignoring her. "Though both men

swear they're not going to be running a race,
Captain Cannon of the *Robt. E. Lee* won't take on
any passengers, while for Captain Leathers of the
Natchez it's business as usual. And the people
sailing on his sternwheeler—statesmen, planters,
bankers and such—will be burdened down with so
much money that they'll welcome the opportunity
to turn it over to us."

Teresa laughed. "Heck, Lamb. I think I'm falling
in love with you."

Hanover smiled.

"Ah, darling, what about that man who was
following us? The one we spotted in the woods,
which must have been the one who later caught us
in that dress shop in Wet Prong?"

He straighted his shoulders. "He's no gentleman.
Allowing a woman to come to his aid."

"That's not what I mean, Lambert! Just suppose
we didn't scare him off? What if he's on the road
right now following us? And who is he anyway? He
didn't look like a Kansas City policeman."

He sighed. "Tessa, there's no use in worrying
about the impossible. I hit his head so hard he'll be
flat on his back for a week. By that time we'll be
on the *Natchez* steaming toward St. Louis. The boat
won't stop for anything except to refuel, so we'll be
safe and he'll be stuck down here. Don't fret your
pretty little head, Tessa."

She frowned. "Maybe, but I still think you should
have let me kill him." Teresa patted the derringer
she'd stuck into her bodice. "Honestly, Lambert, I
don't understand why you won't use firearms!"

Hanover closed his eyes. "My dear, we've dis-
cussed this time and again. I *am* a gentleman.
Gentleman don't soil themselves with gunpowder

or blood."

Teresa stared at the monotonous passing of thousands of green leaved trees. "But I like to do it. What does that make me?"

"A lady. A lady who's handy with weapons. And a very able partner who's saved my hide more than once." He smiled and drove on.

A half-hour before the sun set they came upon a small Cajun village. Teresa turned up her nose at such spartan lodgings so Lambert pushed the horse harder. They made it to a civilized farmhouse just as the western sky deepened into black and the stars popped out above their buggy.

"You must be all tuckered out," a friendly farmer said as he greeted them at his door.

"We are indeed. Could you put us up for the night?" Hanover draped an arm around Teresa's shoulders. "Me and my new bride?"

"Sure! Put the horse in the stable. I'll get your room ready." The man's face was lined and sunburned. "I—I haven't had much company since my wife passed on last year. All I got to remember her by is a gold locket."

Teresa beamed.

Two hours later, Spur was still riding. The buggy tracks had continued with no apparrent stops. For a while or so they'd been overlayed with three or four other sets made by different buggys, but Spur could pick out the narrower, better-made tracks that Hanover's rig had made. He stopped every now and then to ensure that he was still on the right road.

Spur McCoy had no idea where he was, and hadn't seen a town since early that morning. It was nearing dusk, so he figured he'd be sleeping under the stars again.

He found a likely spot and dismounted. The sorrel drank. As night fell around him an eerie fog rolled in. Some distance from him it seemed to glow with an internal light. Must be a big city out there in the distance, he thought, but the flatness of the land made it impossible to see.

He'd find out in the morning.

CHAPTER EIGHT

The old plantation house had seen better days, Teresa Salvare thought as her partner directed the buggy down its long, tree-lined avenue. The glorious pillars that supported the porch, which was level with the roof of the two-story structure, were pitted. One had completely collapsed and lay in massive blocks across the dead lawn.

But she hadn't argued when Lambert had suddenly wanted to stop. It was too tempting. Teresa knew that behind the house lay the fields which may or may not still be bursting with well tended crops. Their condition could indicate whether the owners of the plantation outside of Baton Rouge had held onto their riches, or had lost everything in the ravages of the Civil War.

Before the house, on the other side of the road, lay the wide, slow moving Mississippi River. White steam and black smoke trailed from the stacks of a huge paddleboat as it glided along the water. Not far from it, ten sweating men stood on a cotton laden raft.

Teresa shrieked at the sight of the dead dog lying beside the avenue. She grabbed Hanover's arm.

"Lamb, maybe this wasn't such a good idea."

He smiled. "Now, Tessa. Just because they can't keep up their house doesn't mean that they don't have anything worth stealing."

She sighed. The air was drenched with the spicy-sweetness of magnolia blossoms, and the thirty-year-old woman gazed at the ghostly flowers that festooned the trees.

"Well, if nothing else, I can enjoy the perfume." Teresa sighed and looked at the house. "It doesn't seem like anyone's still living there," she said. "No smoke's coming from any of the chimney's. Why, even the cookhouse stack is dead. Let's turn around, Lamb. No sense in wasting our time."

He turned to her. "Maybe you're right," he said. "Just a little further though. Might as well see."

"Oh, alright!" she huffed, and relaxed against the jiggling seatback.

Two minutes later they were much nearer. "Well, at least there're some horses. Someone must be here." Lambert G. Hanover pointed at the five magnificent steeds tied up at the hitching post.

The sound of gunfire within the plantation house made Hanover rein in their buggy's horse. More shots.

"Let's get out of here!" Teresa said.

"I believe you're right."

"Just go!" she shrieked.

The man coerced their tired beast back in the direction from which they'd come. He used his switch with just the right pressure to urge it to move faster, but Teresa grabbed it from his hands and brutally lashed the poor animal.

"Run, goddammit!" she wailed.

The roan took off. Though the avenue was fairly smooth they nearly bounced from their seats as their buggy tore down it. Additional gunshots sounded in the distance behind them. Teresa gripped Hanover's thigh with one hand and urged the horse to run as fast as it could with its heavy load.

The man bent and looked behind him. "No men in sight yet," he said. "Hurry!"

They cleared the avenue, left behind the magnolias and turned onto the main road headed for New Orleans. Teresa limply held up the switch and gasped.

"It's okay now," Hanover said as the complaining horse instantly settled into an easy gait.

"I told you it was a mistake," she said bitterly. "If we'd turned around when I mentioned it—"

"We'd have been on the road a few minutes earlier. You're right. I should have relied on your feminine intuition."

"Dern right you should have! Hasn't it gotten us out of trouble more than once?"

"Yes. Are we agreed? No more jobs until we reach New Orleans."

She nodded. "Fine, Lamb. Whatever you say."

Not long after they'd gotten to the wagon road five men flashed by them, riding hard, torsos bent toward their horse's pumping necks. Teresa shivered at the thought of what they'd left behind them.

But she had to fight off the urge to go back and see for herself. Teresa imagined the dying bodies oozing blood. The thought made her all warm inside.

Spur shook his head and walked out of the dilapidated plantation house. The whole family had been gunned down. He'd followed the buggy tracks up to the house but had been curious as to why the pair he'd been following had turned back without going in. Once there he saw the reason.

The hoof prints showed that five men had probably done the work. Some local trouble, he figured. Hanover and Teresa weren't involved.

Judging from the tracks, he was still at least a half-day behind them. He was a few miles out of Baton Rouge. They were well on their way to New Orleans. What were they after? Just more con artistry, more money to swell their already bursting collection of illegally gained earnings? Or something bigger?

Spur sighed and rode from the plantation. He had to find them, capture them, and take them into custody alive. That was the hardest part, though he didn't mind admiting that the last thing he wanted to do was to kill a woman.

What irritated him the most was that he couldn't quite picture Teresa's face. He did remember thinking that he'd never forget it—but he had.

He cursed, spat and pushed on beside the broad Mississippi River.

"At last!" Teresa Salvare said.
New Orleans spread before them like a jewel. The river glittered in the sunlight as it bent around the famous town. Steamers, barges, rafts and keelboats littered its surface. Everything from cotton to

merchants and their families were being carted up and down the Mississippi River. The air was heavy with the scents of thousands of flowers mixed with the smell of rotting fish on the banks beside the road.

"Let's find the best hotel in town and get settled in as soon as possible."

"I heartily agree, Lamb," Teresa said, her eyes shining. "I thought we'd never get here."

"Try to think of it this way," Hanover twirled on the tip of his black Van Dyke beard. "Since we've arrived here a week later than we'd originally planned, there are that many more rich people who've come into town. That much more cash and stocks ready for the taking. Many more easy targets for our work. Does that cheer you up?"

"Of course! I wasn't complaining, Lamb."

"Of course. My mistake." He shot her a grin and guided the buggy down the winding, narrow streets.

Hundreds of people littered the wrought-iron porches of the homes. Faces of every color and mixture of races stared out onto a gasping city as the heat and humidity of the day increased to an almost unbearable degree. They were blocked at an intersection by the passing of a funeral procession. Mournful music and the cries of the bereaved mixed with the neighing of horses and the clanging of a nearby church bell tower.

Once the way was clear again, Lambert G. Hanover guided their exhausted horse down a few more streets until one hostelry caught his eye.

"That's a likely place, isn't it?" he asked his female companion.

When she didn't respond, Hanover glanced at her. Teresa was staring at the eye-catching jewelry worn by a well-fed dowager as she stepped from a carriage.

"Tessa!" he said.

"What is it?" She didn't break her gaze.

"Haven't you learned yet? Jewelry is poison. It's too hard to be rid of. Money is simple, clean and neat. It can be spent anywhere with no questions asked. Diamonds and all that are for petty thieves."

She lowered her head and sighed. "Okay, Lamb. You're right. But I couldn't let her walk by without admiring her fine adornments."

"Fine adornments!" Hanover grunted. "My dear, you were thinking of bolting from the buggy, grabbing them from around her thick neck, jumping back in and switching our poor horses to death in a vain attempt to flee! Am I wrong?"

Teresa Salvare crookedly smiled. "You know me too well, Lamb. Far too well."

He laughed as he stepped down from the buggy and helped the woman onto the dusty street. "The Hollister seems like a fine hotel. But remember—we don't do anything here."

"I know. Too dangerous. I'm not a child, after all!"

"I guess I forget, sometimes," he said as he unloaded their considerable baggage and they stepped into the luxuriously appointed inn.

The sky was dark by the time Spur dragged into New Orleans. Exhausted, all he wanted to do was to bed down for the night, but the first five hotels he tried were full. As he walked into the sixth, the Hollister, and got the same answer from the well-dressed night clerk, Spur stomped on the ground.

"Aren't there any rooms available in town?" he asked.

The tight-lipped man shrugged. "I don't know. It's especially busy right now, 'cause of the race."

Spur shook his head, stormed out and rode to the next nearest hotel. It was fancy but he didn't mind that much. A woman in white linen smiled as he walked up to the counter.

"A room for the night, sir?" she asked, purposely taking in his face.

He couldn't hide his surprise. "You have rooms available?"

"Of course, sir! Frankly, we're the most expensive hotel in town. Even the well-to-do folks are staying in less costly lodgings. They're saving their money for the race, I suppose."

"Fine."

He signed the register. "What are the charges?"

"Ten dollars a night, sir?"

Spur didn't even react to the enormous sum that she'd mentioned. He simply fished out $30 and handed the gold pieces to the woman. "Might as well pay in advance," he said.

The lovely innkeeper laughed and stashed the money in her cash drawer. "Mighty obliged to you. Room 14." She handed him a key, dangling it from a slender, white hand.

He nodded, grabbed the key and walked up the stairs, ready for a night of doing nothing but sleeping and dreaming.

Though he didn't turn up the kerosene lamps, Spur saw that the room was outrageously luxurious. But the lawman was too tired to care. Moonlight flooded the room from the window, and all he could see as he walked in and locked the door behind him was the bed. It looked good. Real good. Even empty it was the prettiest thing he'd ever seen.

Spur chucked his clothes and dumped them on the Persian carpets that covered the floor, pulled off his boots and socks and flopped onto the pigeon feather mattress.

He worked a kink out of his neck and enjoyed the comparative coolness of the sheets. Soon, however, the humidity of the town beside the river crept into his room and made him sweat profusely. Cursing, Spur rose and went to the windows. He opened them, allowing a light breeze to filter in.

As he stretched out again the wind chilled him. It took him several minutes to drift off to sleep. As he laid there he heard a man and a woman in the room next door arguing.

Something about a race . . . .

CHAPTER NINE

Teresa Salvare slowly moved the boar bristle brush through her hair, lovingly caressing each blonde strand. Sitting before the window as the early morning breeze blew through the city of New Orleans, she gazed down at the street and smiled.

The town was bustling beneath her. Everyone in the city seemed to be out during the coolest part of the day. She lost count of the number of expensive carriages and well-dressed people who passed below her hotel window.

Teresa felt a warm hand press against her shoulder.

"Good morning."

"Lamb," she said. "You finally got up."

He yawned. "What are you looking at out there?" The man, wrapped in a brocade robe, bent and put his head near hers, peering through the window.

"What am I looking at? Why, the riches of New Orleans! What else would I—I—" She threw down the brush. "Lamb! I don't believe it!"

"What?"

"Look. There! That man!"

"Which one? Honey, there must be at least a hundred men in sight."

"You fool! The one in the brown Stetson! Right there! He's turning back. He's walking into our hotel!"

"I'll be damned. I'll be goddamned!"

Teresa blew out her breath. "Am I right?"

"It sure looks like it. That's him. The lawman who caught up with us in Wet Prong."

"What's he doing here?" Teresa demanded. "He doesn't belong here! He belongs six feet under!"

"Calm yourself, Tessa."

She watched him walk out of sight into the hotel, then stood and paced, clutching her elbows. "I told you we should have killed him!"

"That wouldn't have been too easy, with that pistol-packing woman around."

Teresa stopped. "I would have taken care of her too," she snapped. "Or I could have, if only you weren't so scared to use guns. Honestly, Lambert G. Hanover! If I didn't know better I'd think you were—"

He pounced on her, grabbed Teresa's arm and twisted it. "You'd think I was *what*?"

"Stop it! You're hurting me!"

His eyes glazed over. Hanover increased the pressure, staring the woman down. She yelped. The man suddenly released her and faced the wall, his body rigid, arms hanging tightly. "I'm sorry, Tessa."

She rubbed her developing bruises. "Sorry?"

His nostrils flared. "You have no right to talk like that. You know nothing about me—my background, the reason I do things the way I do."

"You never talk about it." The woman retrieved her fallen brush, sat at the window and worked on her yellow hair again. "How could I know?"

"Do you consider me to be a gentleman?"

She smiled at her reflection in the silvered mirror. "Sure, I guess, Lamb. Usually. When you're not trying to twist off my arms."

He sighed. "I was born to a poory family. My father put food on our table by picking pockets. He wasn't above killing his victims after he'd robbed them. We lived in the dirtiest, most downtrodden part of Philadelphia. Mother never spoke of how my father earned his money. I only knew that we managed to get by."

Hanover looked at his partner. "One night I couldn't go to sleep. I'd broken my arm while playing with a friend and it ached and ached. So I heard them talking. We all slept in the same room, you understand." He closed his eyes. "My father was describing his day's activities. When he was through, he bragged that he must have killed fifty men and woman in the last few years. Fifty. He bragged about it, Tessa!"

She stopped brushing and shook her head.

"I hid under my dirty sheet and stayed awake until morning. After my father had left and my mother had walked to the street market, I stole as much money as I could find in the house and ran away. Two days later I was working for the Tompkins, a wealthy family. I did that for years as I grew to be a man. I watched my employers and learned how to act in high society. How to be a gentleman. Eventually, I saved up enough money to buy myself the finest suit that I could find and fell into gambling. From that it was a short trip to stealing—but I never, never used a firearm!"

Teresa sat silently, looking blank-faced at him. "Because you father—"

"Yes! Because my father had killed all those innocent people. Oh, you know that I'm no saint. I love my work, but I'm not about to continue the family tradition."

"Have you seen your family since?"

He shook his head and grabbed a cigar from a table. "No. My mother died from a fever a few years after I left. Later, I heard through friends that my father met his end in a grubby Philadelphia alley not far from Independence Hall, gunned down in cold blood by one of his victims. You see, my father had mistakenly tried to rob a policeman. It was the last thing he ever did."

Hanover bit off the end of the cigar, spat in into a gleaming spitton and lit its tip with a lucifer match. He puffed until it glowed. "So don't talk to me of guns, Teresa. I won't use them. Still, if it should become necessary, to protect our lives—you handle that."

She rose and went to him. Teresa's nostrils flared at the strong scent of cigar smoke. "So I have your permission to kill that man? The one we just saw outside? The one who's here to lock us up and, probably, to have us hanged?"

He puffed and nodded.

Teresa smiled.

That morning, as he stepped from the Hollister Hotel, Spur realized that he'd forgotten breakfast. He continued into the street for a few paces before his stomach grumbled. That settled it. He turned and walked back into the hotel to find the dining room.

This wasn't the rough eating establishment of some frontier town hotel. It was a real restaurant, with fresh flowers and linen on every table, crystal glasses and sterling silver flatware. He got a table near the windows.

The starched-collar waiter took his order and returned almost immediately with a cup of coffee and a small plate of strange round doughnuts. Spur took one bite. The delicious taste made him quickly consume every morsel.

During breakfast, Spur looked at the other diners and realized that he'd underdressed. He had put on a clean pair of riding clothes but still he was plainly out of place in this rich town. Because the pair of thieves he was following usually mixed with the rich folks, the highest class of society, he realized that he'd better change.

After his meal he started up the stairs. A blonde woman was just stepping down them. They met in the middle. She let out a yell and stumbled right into his arms.

Spur easily grabbed the woman's shoulders and held her until she'd righted herself. Fine peach-colored silk crackled beneath his fingers. She smelled of jasmine. The beautiful woman gave him a rueful smile.

"I declare!" she said in an accent that dripped honey. "I just can't get used to this new pair of boots."

"Are you alright, ma'am?" Spur asked as he removed his hat.

"I think I'm fine. Let me see."

She took a tentative step and immediately hurled

forward. "Oh!"

Once again catching the woman, Spur grinned as she raised her right foot behind her. "I knew it! The heel came right off. That cobbler cheated me out of good money!"

The Southern belle spun around her head. Their faces were inches apart. Her breath was laced with mint.

"Kind sir, do you think I could call upon you to help me back to my room? I could never do it alone."

"Of course. Back up stairs?"

"Yes. If it wouldn't be too much of burden on you."

"Not at all."

She placed an arm over his shoulders as they turned on the step. Spur firmly grabbed her waist and guided her back up the ten steps.

"It's room 23, down the hall," she said, and smiled sweetly at him.

Spur certainly didn't mind the distraction. Her body was warm and firm. It bulged beneath the woman's bodice, betraying the presence of her breasts. She felt so good, he thought, as she limped down the hall.

"Here we are! Just push the door open. I'm too trusting to use the lock, or to check new boots before I buy them." The woman gave him a rueful smile.

"Fine."

The door swung open. Spur helped the beautiful woman in her room. Expensive dresses lay in careful piles over virtually every part of it save for the bed, so he guided her to its edge. She lightly sat and smiled up at him.

"Thank you, sir. I never could have done it alone."

"It's no burden helping a pretty lady in distress."

She laughed and unbuttoned her boots. "These sorry things belong in a junk heap! Of all the nerve! That shifty-eyed Italian charged me eleven dollars."

"They'll charge whatever they can get away with." Spur backed to the door.

The woman flashed him a smile. "Why, wherever are you going?" she asked.

"Well, away."

She fluttered her eyelashes. "I thought you said you were going to help me."

Spur grinned. "And I thought you meant up the stairs. Is there something more I can do for you?"

The Southern belle kicked off her boots and stood. "Yes; there is, Yankee. If you'll be so kind as to close the door?"

He quickly did so. "I really should be getting to my work."

The woman smiled and pulled off her bonnet. Golden hair rained down around her face. "And what might that be?"

"Ah—er—"

She arched her back. "You couldn't take out just a few minutes more?"

He stared at the swells of her breasts, her slender waist and the curve of her hips. "Maybe I could." This woman was making the crotch of his pants uncomfortably tight. And she knew exactly how to do it.

"Good. I guess all Yankees aren't alike. My daddy always said they wouldn't lift a finger to help out a woman, especially one from the South."

He approached her. His excitement must have been obvious to her. "Things just aren't that simple.

We're all individuals."

"I see. Do you think you could help me again now?"

"Yes. Anything."

The woman turned around. "I can never reach those buttons on the top of my dress."

Spur McCoy smiled and pulled them free of the cloth flap. As he worked his way down her back, the peach material parted to reveal a cream-colored chemise.

"That's much better!"

He pulled his hands away.

"Oh no! Don't stop! My arm's hurting from that silly tumble I had on the stairs."

"Whatever you say, ma'am." He returned to his work.

"Call me Marie."

He unfastened the last button. "It's done."

"Good."

She turned around, reached into her now sagging bodice and pulled out a pearl-handled derringer.

CHAPTER TEN

Spur backed from her. Teresa Salvare looked down at the derringer she'd just produced, then up at the man. She smiled, laughed and placed the weapon onto the dresser drawer.

"A woman all alone in this city can't be too careful," she said. She watched the man's face unknit. "My daddy, the Colonel, taught me how to use one of those things, but I've never shot anything bigger than a tin can."

"I hope it stays like that." The man's face visibly relaxed. It had been a tense moment or two. "You had me worried there for a second, Marie."

"Really? How odd!" Teresa said, thickening her Southern accent.

"Well, you turned around and showed me a weapon. I'm out on the frontier a lot, not used to these comfortable cities. You meet all kinds of men and women out there. Tough ones. So I was naturally startled. I hope you don't take that as an insult. It was a natural reaction."

She smiled. "Oh, I see." She held her hand briefly over her lips. "I don't think of that pearl-handled beauty as a weapon, necessarily. Most times it's just a dadblamed nuisance, jabbed between my—you know. But I never got out on the street without it." Teresa played the role to the hilt. She called on every acting lesson she'd ever received.

"It pays to be careful. Especially in a town of this size." He took off his hat. "Where were we?"

"Oh yes, I remember." She slipped down the left shoulder of her dress. "You were about to do me another favor. What I hope will be a *big* favor."

He laughed. "I don't get many complaints. Marie, you're absolutely intoxicating."

"Really?" she asked as she slipped off the other side of her dress. Her stretched chemise popped into view.

"Your face, your lovely body, even your voice. It's getting me so excited that I can't be held accountable for my actions."

"So who's counting?"

Spur pulled off his boots. "Are you sure you're all alone? No one will come barging in here, will they?"

She laughed. "Of course not!"

As they undressed, Teresa kept smiling. The moment simply hadn't been right. She had surprised him, yes, but he still had his holster and his own weapon. If he was a professional lawman he could easily outdraw her. Even before she'd finished aiming and firing he would have shot her.

So she'd had to change her course of plans. Bedding him was one way to ensure that his Colt .45 was far out of reach. She thought about how she'd prepared for this, concealing weapons of various types around the room.

Of course, he wasn't bad looking, Teresa thought. She was particularly attracted to his strong jaw, piercing eyes, and, now that she saw it, his hairy chest. The lawman grinned at her and dropped his pants and underdrawers. The enormous proof of his masculinity swung up between his legs and reached for the sky.

She gasped and slapped her breast. "My!" Teresa said. "I have a feeling you're going to be doing me a very big favor!"

Spur laughed.

Lambert G. Hanover cursed as he paced Chartre Street, dodging aged women, French-spouting priests, quadroon children and a host of other everyday folks. He'd walked there, some four blocks distant from the hotel, because he didn't want to be involved in Teresa's plan in any way—not even to hear the deed being done.

He knew she was safe enough. The lawman hadn't recognized her as they'd met on the stairs—Hanover had stayed long enough to watch that much of the proceedings—and she was a crack shot, better than many men he'd known.

And despite his deep-seated distaste for violence, he'd had to agree with her plan. Hanover was smart enough to realize that with the lawman out of the way their stay in New Orleans and the trip up the Mississippi would be that much pleasanter.

"Bananas! Sweet yellow bananas!" a street vendor called as she pushed a wooden wheeled cart down Chartre. "Buy my sweet yellow bananas!"

"Hey!" he yelled.

The vendor hurried to him. "You want buy my banana?" she asked him.

"Yes, my good woman. How much?"

"Ten cents a finger." She licked her lips as he removed his money clip.

"How much for a whole bunch?" Hanover asked.

She widened her eyes and pulled at the scarf that covered her frizzy black hair. "Oh, sir, they come all the way from the Antilles. Captain just brought them into port. Sweet and eating-ready."

"Fine. fine!" he said as he studied the strange, exotic fruit. He caught a whiff of its odor. "Just tell me how much you want for a whole bunch!"

She picked one up. "You taste before?"

"Once, in Boston. Woman, give me your final price or be gone!"

"Okay, okay. Ten bananas, dollar-fifty."

He pulled two dollar bills from his money clip and handed them to the fruit vendor, took the bunch and walked stiffly from her. Before he turned the corner he heard her plaintive call:

"Bananas! Sweet yellow bananas! Buy my sweet yellow bananas!"

Lambert G. Hanover walked quickly down the winding streets until he came to Jackson Square. Across from the barouque St. Louis' Cathedral, he found a wrought-iron bench, tore off one of the costly fruits and examined it.

Now all he had to do was to remember how to get the fruit out.

Spur smiled as the woman stood stark naked before him.

"Do you still think I'm a lady?" she asked, perfectly comfortable in her exposed condition.

He took in her beautiful body and swallowed hard. "Marie, after seeing all of you I'd say you're definitely a lady. All lady."

"That's not what I mean," she said. Her breasts bounced as she walked toward him. "I mean a cultured, classy lady. One you'd accept into the finest homes."

"Sure! I guess. It's sort of hard to tell without any clothes on."

"I know. That's why I like it this way." She rubbed her right nipple.

Spur's erection throbbed even harder before him.

The woman smiled. "I don't believe I caught your name, Yankee."

"McCoy, Marie. Spur McCoy."

"Well, then, Spur, come to bed. You'll find out just how much of a lady I am!"

He laughed and sat on the velvet-covered mattresses.

"You coming too?"

"Of course. But I almost forgot to shut the drapes. Don't want anyone looking in from across the street."

The woman pulled them, blocking out the intense morning sunlight. The room darkened considerably, cutting off a clear view of her deliciously round bottom.

"Now we're all set." She went to the bed.

Spur edged over to give her room. The woman faced away from him, spread out her arms and fell directly onto the mattress on her back. "Take me!" she said.

Aroused by the woman's undisguised desire, at her bold willingness to reveal her true feelings, the Secret Service agent didn't think twice about it. He rolled on top of her and kissed her.

"No preliminaries? Just do it?" he asked.

"Yes. Now! Spur, I'm wet. And I'm on fire."

She reached between their bodies and gripped him. He moaned at the sensuous feeling of her hand. She lifted her knees and parted them, opening herself.

"You're the boss," he said. Spur positioned himself and thrust into the very willing woman.

She gasped and shivered. Spur pushed deeper. She arched her back and raked his flesh with her fingernails. He drove in full length and grabbed her shoulders as their bodies were fully connected.

"Jesus!" she said. "I mean, that's what I like!"

"Come on." Spur nuzzled her neck. "You can drop the act now."

She went stiff below him. "What ever do you mean?"

Spur laughed. "I know you're not a lady, though you act like one. But I don't like ladies. Just say whatever you feel like saying. I won't tell anyone. Okay?"

"Okay. I guess I don't have any choice."

"Tell me how this feels."

He reared back and plunged into her. The woman shivered and shook as their pubic bones crashed together. She was a mystery, Spur thought as he began the slow, rhythmic pumping that man and woman had enjoyed since the beginning of time.

But there was no mystery about her reaction to the hot sex. Marie bucked and writhed beneath him, crumpling the exquisitely expensive velvet comforter. She dug her fingernails into his back.

"Faster. Faster!" she said.

When his pace didn't satisfy her, she grabbed his

buttocks and pulled them back and forth, deeply impaling herself on his penis, furiously trying to bring her body to an intense explosion.

The woman dropped all pretenses, Spur thought, though he was barely capable of organizing his mind. Her blonde hair swirled like an unholy halo around her head. She constantly moistened her lips between low moans and urged him to go as hard and as fast as he could.

Guttural pants blasted from between Spur's lips. Their bodies banged together. He looked down at her furry mound and pounded into her with twice the strength as before.

"Oh heck. Oh hell! Goddamn it, Spur! Spur! SPUR!"

Her hands slapped against his sweating lower back. She locked her fingers and pulled him back and forth, shaking and spasming. The old cherrywood bed creaked and groaned under their shifting weight. Spur held onto the woman to maintain their connection as she kicked and fought her way through the blinding experience.

"Jesus, Marie!"

He didn't even think of holding back as his scrotum contracted. Her undisguised passion soon led to his own, and Spur drained himself in a series of animalistic thrusts mixed with grunts. Every muscle in his body flexed and tightened with each brain-numbing spurt.

Their trembling bodies swayed on the bed. The woman's passion subsided before Spur's. He maintained the heated contact as the last few tremors shot through his being.

The blonde woman relaxed and draped a hand over his back. Spur slumped onto her, putting his full weight on the delicate woman. He kissed her neck between his gasps.

The room was suddenly incredibly hot but Spur couldn't do anything about it. He was helpless, spent, his mind whirling with thoughts about this beautiful woman who'd brought him to the peak of the human experience.

She sighed and rubbed his shoulders, her fingers tracing the still tense muscles that she found there. Spur smiled as she hummed a tune.

"I'm sorry," he said. "I must be crushing you. Here, let me move off."

"No, you're not crushing me at all. Well, maybe you are, but I like it. Stay right there, Spur!"

He nodded. "Okay."

Their lips met. It was a sweet, lingering kiss, drained of all passion. Her soft mouth and cheeks, the way she darted her tongue against his, excited Spur all over again. He wasn't exactly surprised to feel new life returning to his still buried penis.

She broke the kiss and regarded him with raised eyebrows. "My word, sir. Again?"

He nodded. "Unless you're too much of a lady."

Marie laughed out loud.

The first banana had been delicious. Hanover found it to be slightly mushy, but that was to be expected. After all, the fruit had travelled by schooner for two weeks to reach the port of New Orleans.

The second was even better, and before he knew it Lambert G. Hanover had eaten three of the expensive fruits. He threw down the peel, dabbed at the corners of his mouth with a handkerchief and stood. Clutching the remaining fruit, he left the bench and leisurely strolled through New Orleans.

He realized that this wasn't Kansas City. It wasn't a raw city but one steeped in history that was written even before Jefferson's historic Louisiana Purchase. The French had been there in force. Several other nations had grappled for control of New Orleans and the prize that lay behind it—the Mississippi River and its avenue to riches.

As he walked by St. Louis Cathedral he passed a large dark-skinned woman. She held her chin proudly and her voluminous white cotton dress billowed in the breeze. Her lips moved with a soundless, continuous chanting.

He was about to dismiss her as a harmless crank when Hanover happened to look down. The man was shocked to see two snakes coiled comfortably around her arms.

He stumbled over a stone. The woman halted and slowly turned to face him. She took in his surprised face and fancy clothes.

"The blessings of St. John and Ellegua on you, my child," she said, and walked off.

Though Hanover had certainly heard of it in legends, he hadn't expected so see much of it during his short stay in the city. But there it was, plain as day.

Voodoo.

• After the second time, Teresa Salvare was truly exhausted. She lay beside the panting man for several minutes until she'd regained her wits.

He stirred as she sat and put her feet on the floor.

"Going somewhere?" he asked.

She patted his hairy stomach. "Just to get a glass of water. You want anything?"

"Mmmmm."

She shook her head and walked to the pitcher that stood on an elaborately carved table. Once there, though, Teresa stared into the empty basin and sighed. It seemed such a terrible waste. He was so handsome, strong and intelligent. Such an incredible lover. To top it all off, he had the biggest one she'd ever seen—certainly far more impressive than Lambert's tool.

But she faced facts. He was the enemy, she told herself. And the enemy had to die. Teresa looked around the room. She saw the derringer where she'd placed it. She thought about the knife under the mattress and the packet of poison she'd placed beneath the whiskey bottle.

What should she use?

"Marie?"

His throaty voice broke into her thoughts. "Yes, my love?"

"I think you took off two inches."

She spontaneously laughed and realized it was no act. "Spur, it takes two people, remember? I certainly didn't do it all alone."

"Okay. I'm too tired to argue."

Teresa turned and saw him settle on the bed. His head flopped away from her.

He trusted her completely. He couldn't have recognized her. If he had, the lawman wouldn't have allowed himself to be placed in such a helpless position.

He was such an easy mark. Then why couldn't she kill him?

Teresa firmed her resolve. She went to the table where they kept the liquor.

"I'll never move again," he said from the bed.

"I know just what you need. A touch of whiskey."
She slipped the folded paper from beneath the
bottle and sprinkled its white contents into a glass.
Teresa's hands shook as she opened the whiskey
and poured it into the glass. The powder dissolved
and was soon invisible.

That done, she poured her own glass, replaced the
cork in the whiskey bottle and carefully took Spur's
glass in her right hand. Picking up her own, she
walked to the bed.

"Come on," she said. "Take a drink. It'll make you
feel better."

"I'm asleep," Spur said, yawning.

"It'll do you good, honey. Put some life back into
your veins." She tapped his shoulder.

Grumbling, he flipped over. His head comically
landed on the dented pillow. Spur extended a hand.

Teresa Salvare gave him the drink that contained
the poison. She raised her own glass. "To . . . sex!"
she said with forced brightness.

He nodded and raised the tumbler to his lips.

CHAPTER ELEVEN

Spur hesitated and looked into his glass of whiskey. Drinking hard liquor so early in the morning wasn't his idea of starting the day out right. But was it still early? The room was so dark with the curtains closed that he had no idea of the time.

Still, a bit would be a good bracer. The woman hadn't begun drinking yet either. Spur shrugged.

"Aren't you going to take a sip at least?" she said.

"What are you, a daughter of a whiskey manufacturer trying to increase your old pappy's profits?"

"Hardly!" Marie said. "I just think you might . . . you know, need it. After all the work you just did. I mean, that we both did."

He gazed into the amber-colored liquid. "I guess a little wouldn't kill me."

Marie's smile faded. She downed the contents of her drink and turned her tumbler upside down.

"My dear, you're trying to make me a drunkard."

He rested the rim of the glass against his lower lip.

The beautiful, naked woman suddenly bounced up and down on the bed. The movement made Spur's arm wobble wildly, which spilled his whiskey all over the mattress.

"Oh dear!" she said, quickly grabbing the now empty glass from his hand and spiriting it away to the table. "Look what I've done! I'm sorry." She returned to the bed. "I guess I was just so eager for you to take a drink, thinking it might put you in the mood again—"

"Again!" Spur said, dabbing at the two dribbles of whiskey that had landed on his chest.

"—that I was impatient. So I started jumping up and down like a little girl." She ruefully smiled. "That shows me that sometimes it's better to act like a cultured, genteel lady instead of the hot-blooded woman I am."

Spur grinned and looked down at the whiskey-soaked comforter. "If you were simply preparing me for another roll in the hay, Marie, you might have just saved my life."

Her gaze found his. "What?" The woman shook her head in confusion.

"One more with you would have been the death of me." He slapped at his limp organ.

She laughed and grabbed a towel. "I guess I better clean up that nasty spill," she said.

"And I probably should be getting dressed." He looked down at his chest. "Care to lick that liquor off my chest?" he asked with a leer.

The blonde haired woman held out a hand. "I—I—no, Spur. I don't think so. Not only would I get lost in that fur of yours, but I already had a full glass. That's enough to last me until December 25th!"

"Okay." He grabbed a corner of her towel and wiped himself dry as she rubbed the ruined velvet comforter.

Lambert G. Hanover looked up at his hotel window and frowned. She still hadn't opened the drapes, which meant that the man was still in their room and probably alive. A sudden thought bothered him, so he pulled out his money clip.

He had more than enough. Hanover walked across the street, dodging a speeding carriage and two men on horseback, and stepped into the barber shop.

"I need a shave," he said, fingering his Van Dyke beard as the squat barber looked up at him.

"Okay, okay. Hold your horses. So much damn work all the time," the barber said as he grabbed a pair of rusty scissors.

Perhaps the lawman hadn't remembered what Teresa looked like, but he couldn't count on that being true of himself. He could have described him to the local police. Might as well change his appearance.

"Cut too?"

Hanover shook his head. "Ah, what?"

"I asked if you wanted a cut too?"

He shook his head. Settling into the chair, half-listening to the barber's unintelligible banter, Hanover wondered what color his hair should be this month. Brown? Red?

He smiled. Red it would be.

"I'm awfully grateful for you help," Teresa Salvare said as she saw Spur to her hotel room door. "For everything."

He touched the brim of his hat. "Nothing any red-blooded American wouldn't do for a lady in distress. Sorry I have to leave, but business is waiting for me."

She smiled. "I understand. I have to look after some of my own affairs." She kissed his cheek, patted his behind and scooted him out the door. "See you around, Spur!"

She closed and locked the door. Teresa sighed and looked at the window. She should open the curtains to alert Lambert, but the last thing she wanted to do was to face him. She had no idea how he'd react. Would he be happy? Furious? It was too much to think about.

She turned up one of the kerosene lamps and tidied up the room, selected one of her good pairs of boots from the free-standing closet and put them on. Cutting off the heel of one of another pair had been a small sacrifice to lure the handsome lawman into her hotel room, but now it just seemed silly.

In the past, Teresa had killed men with firearms. She'd always done it quickly with little or no time for thought before pulling the trigger that released the hammer and the speeding death.

But this had been something different. Deliberately setting out to murder a man and then carrying out the plan had proved to be impossible, especially while she was still basking in the glow of their recent exertions on the stained bed.

The first time he'd hesitated to drink the poisoned whiskey Teresa was startled to realize that she didn't want him to down it, that she wanted him to live. By the time he'd finally relented and raised his glass again she'd had the uncontrollable urge to do something, anything to stop him from killing himself. So she'd bounced on the bed as hard as she could.

It had worked. He was still alive and now gone, lost somewhere in the city. The paddleboat race was still a day away. What would she and Lambert do until tomorrow?

Teresa wearily stood, went to the window and opened the drapes. Then she sat beside the dark-colored spot on the velvet comforter, waiting to give her partner in crime the bad news.

Frustrated at his lack of progress in tracking the thieving couple in bustling New Orleans, Spur leaned against the corner of a pastel pink building. Bored and hot, he turned and read the notices that had been plastered all over the flat surface. There were signs trumpeting the arrival of medicine men, of revival meetings to be held next Sunday beside the Mississippi, of an upcoming ball. But one notice caught Spur's full attention.

A CARD TO THE PUBLIC

Reports have been circulating through the city that the great steamer NATCHEZ is intending to engage in a race at 5:04 P.M. June 30th. Such reports are untrue. All passengers may leave with her on that day in the knowledge that the steamer NATCHEZ will be be racing any other craft on Thursday, June 30th, but will be making its regularly scheduled trip to St. Louis.

T. P. Leathers, Master
Steamer Natchez

Spur smiled as he read the public notice. Despite the captain's carefully worded announcement, it was obvious that a race was on. He realized that everywhere he'd gone that afternoon people had been talking about the race.

McCoy stopped at the nearest saloon and listened to several conversations. Men bragged of how much they were betting, and they weren't talking about the great wheel of fortune that stood in one corner of the dingy little saloon.

"The *Robert E. Lee* is the fastest steamer afloat!" one red-faced man yelled.

The man sitting at the table with him guffawed and scratched his bald head. "You're full of beans, Fletcher! The *Natchez* can beat old Cannon's leaky barge any day!"

"Ten bucks says it can't!"

"Twenty dollars says it can!"

"Boys, boys," a suited man said as he slapped the pair on their backs. "Why don't you start talking about real money? I have $1,000 on the *Natchez*."

"You hear that, George?" Fletcher asked his drinking partner. "Caron here's going to be dead broke in a few days."

"Now see here, Fletcher!" George began.

"Fuck you!"

They pushed back their chairs. A fistfight broke out. Spur had heard enough. He wandered outside into the intense heat.

The first man he passed was taking bets. So too were several others. New Orleans had gone crazy with the fever of a steamboat race up the great Mississippi River.

"You what?" Lambert G. Hanover roared.

Teresa lunged toward him from across the room at the Hollister Hotel. "You heard me, I couldn't do it! I thought you'd be happy, Lambert, since you'd probably rather wait for a chicken to die before you'd shoot it for your supper!"

"I never asked you to shoot him!"

Teresa pushed back her shoulders. "I did poison his whiskey but he didn't drink it. That's in the past. So what do we do now?"

He paced. "It's the 29th. If we can hide out somewhere tonight, and board the *Natchez* just before she leaves, he'll never find us again."

"That's just what I was thinking." Teresa poured herself another drink. "So where can we go?"

"I'm sure we can find a party to attend. I heard of a few happening tonight."

"Fine. Then go out there and do what you know how to do best! Give them some sweet talk and get an invitation! I'll start packing."

"No. First we move to another hotel, then we think about this evening. I'm not sure that this Spur McCoy is registered here, but he knows where you're staying. That's dangerous enough."

"Okay!" She exploded with activity, throwing dresses and hats into her leather luggage. "Let's pack!"

"You never should have let him go, Teresa," Lambert said as he quietly folded his best suit.

She flashed him a fast smile. "That's just what I was telling you the other day. I'll never hear the end of this, will I?"

Hanover exploded. "Damn you, woman!" he shouted. The veins popped out of his neck. "You say you're as tough as any man but when it comes right down to it you can't do the one thing that—that—" he paused and bent closer to the bed. "Teresa! What's this stain on the comforter?"

Her face colored. "That's the whiskey that he didn't drink," she said.

Lambert G. Hanover faced her. "On the bed? You were on the bed with him?"

She nodded.

"And he took you, didn't he? Didn't he?"

Teresa waved off his question. "Yes! I figured it would distract him!"

Hanover laughed. "It must have distracted you, too. Okay. I'll hate myself for this, but you've forced me to come to a decision. If we ever run into the man again, I'll cut him down myself before he can blink an eye."

"With what?"

"With the firearm I intend to buy as soon as we're out of this hotel," he said evenly.

She started to laugh but withheld the urge. Sweet, cultured Lamb kill a man? She couldn't picture it. "I'll believe that when I see it."

Teresa caught the long yellow object that Hanover threw at her. "What is it?"

"What does it remind you of?" He leered.

"Ah—well—"

"Never mind. It's a banana."

She turned it over in her hands. "It's food, right? Do you eat it?"

"Yes. But I don't suppose you'd want one right now. Not after that lawman's banana."

She huffed and returned to her packing.

CHAPTER TWELVE

Spur leaned against a lamp post. He ignored the fact that his clothes were hanging from his body, soaked with the sweat that New Orleans' impossible humidity had produced.

The dampness of the air wasn't the only thing impossible. Spur had no idea of how to find Lambert G. Hanover and Teresa, the thieves he'd been following for over three weeks now. He'd stopped in at 12 saloons. He'd gone to dozens of women's dress shops and millioners. And he'd found nothing.

Surely they were in New Orleans. Their trail had headed this way and it seemed the perfect place for the con artists to ply their trade, with all the conspicuous wealth of the rich port town waiting to be taken into their greedy, thieving hands.

But where were they? As he leaned against the kerosene lamp post down by the river and stared at the dozens of people who passed, Spur realized the enormity of his task. Finding the two among the 150,000 or so souls who inhabited New Orleans wasn't going to be easy.

All he had to go on were the cryptic descriptions that his boss, General Halleck, had sent him. Sure, he'd seen them briefly, but he couldn't remember their faces.

Spur removed his Stetson and rubbed the two lumps that sat on the top of his head. They were still tender but were obviously healing. The swelling had gone down. He had to admire Hanover's sense of placement—he'd hit him just where it would make his brain so disoriented that the whole incident was somewhat cloudy in his mind.

On the street before him, a short, stocky man lugged a huge basket on his back. Inside it, hundreds of crablike creatures flexed their pincers and wriggled around.

"Crawfish! Buy my live crawfish!" the street vendor said in a plaintive cry.

Spur sighed and slapped his wounds. The pain seemed to jolt something inside him. Encouraged, he tried to remember exactly what had happened in Wet Prong, to recreate the whole agonizing scene.

He remembered the shop. He remembered the woman with the dress pulled over her face, hiding it but showing off her underclothing. He remembered the store owner demanding that he leave. Then the crushing blow that had come from behind him and which had sent him reeling to the floor and momentarily blacked out!

Okay so far, he thought.

Spur recalled coming out of it, groggy but fairly conscious. The woman pulled down her dress. She'd argued with the man. Spur had still been on the floor, flat on his back, but he'd seen both Hanover and Teresa. *What did they look like?*

The woman had wanted to kill him, but the man stated that he'd simply break Spur's legs. His words came back to him.

"You know how hard it is to ride a horse with a broken leg?" Hanover had said.

Then the shopkeeper had threatened the con artists with a six-gun. The pair of thieves had made themselves scarce in a hurry.

What came after that wasn't important, at least not for his purposes, so he went back over the scene. Nothing more. No details of Hanover's and Teresa's appearance. All he could remember was that she had long blonde hair.

Frustrated, Spur slapped the top of his head again. The new pain firmed his resolve. He tried to picture her. The yellow hair . . . the soft chin . . . the blue eyes . . .

Spur panted. Was he doing it? Was he finally remembering her?

She was beautiful. A perfect, short nose, flawless skin, luscious lips and a body with curves in all the right places.

Confusion swirled in his mind. Was that Teresa, or was that the woman he'd spent a few hours with earlier that morning? The one who'd broken her heel on the stairs in the hotel?

Spur rubbed his forehead. Which woman was it? The more he thought about it, the simpler it was. It was both.

Teresa, the thief from Kansas City, was Marie, the woman he'd bedded.

The thought struck McCoy like lightning. It couldn't be. Could it? Yes it could. She'd lured him to her hotel room with the story of the broken heel—that was easy enough to prepare if she'd known he was staying there too.

Once in her room, Marie/Teresa had showed him her derringer. Had she meant to fire it, to kill him? If so, why hadn't she just done it?

They'd made love twice. She was so willing, so exciting, so totally involved that he couldn't believe she knew he was the lawman who'd been following her and her partner.

He shook his head. It didn't make sense. Teresa would have simply killed him and been done with it. Unless . . . unless she had been toying with him, showing that she didn't consider him to be a real threat.

"Fuck!" he said aloud, startling a flock of birds and three small boys who were walking by with popguns. They turned angry faces at him; he'd alerted their potential prey.

Spur flew down the street. He dodged the endless procession of buggies, carriages, riders and people of every race walking the heated streets. He gasped the liquid air, breathing in the aromas of sausage, fresh fish, horse droppings and cheap perfume. His boots pounded the dust.

A buggy was just pulling away from it as he neared the Hollister Hotel. Spur surged in front of it and stopped, forcing it to halt as well. When he saw the driver—an aged black woman—Spur smiled and waved her on.

Then into the hotel. He didn't bother with the front desk but took the steps two at a time up the stairs. On the landing he headed for room 23. The door easily opened.

The room was empty. The piles of dresses were

gone. No personal articles were in sight. Spur cursed and took one last look around the room.

He found an ashtray on an inlaid table. The butt of a cigar was propped onto it. Lambert G. Hanover must have stayed out of sight while his lady was entertaining Spur.

McCoy huffed. He couldn't believe the woman had tricked him! How could he have been so blind, not to see that the very thief he'd been looking for had taken him to bed?

And why hadn't she killed him? If he was right—and everything pointed to it—Teresa/Marie should have blown him to bits. But she hadn't. Why not?

Spur stared down at the mattress and saw the amber-colored stain that marred the velvet comforter. He remembered that after they'd screwed two times she had urged him to drink some whiskey. It seemed strange that a woman would want her man to drink so early in the morning, but she'd been so insistent that he'd finally given in.

Then Teresa/Marie had bounced the bed so hard that he'd spilled the entire contents of his glass. He'd thought it was odd at the time but now it seemed even odder.

And she wouldn't lick off the few drops that had splattered on his chest.

Poison? It seemed likely. Teresa had almost tried to do him in with the derringer but had quickly decided against it. Perhaps the fact that he had still been armed had changed her mind. Then she'd slipped poison into his whiskey but had made it impossible for him to drink it.

Perhaps she wasn't the cold-blooded killer she'd made herself out to be in Wet Prong. Perhaps she had a sense of right and wrong.

Or maybe she'd simply lost her nerve.

Spur rubbed the stain.

"Lordy!" a woman said behind him.

He turned to watch a black maid walk in, her arms filled with fresh sheets.

"What are you doing in here? They told me this room needed to be made up."

"It does. Sorry."

He went down the stairs and banged on the bell at the front desk. This finally produced the manager, a thin, tall, white-haired man who slipped into his coat as he appeared from the office.

"Can I help you, sir?"

"I hope so. I'm registered in room twenty-four. My friends were staying in twenty-three. We were supposed to leave together today, but their room seems to be empty."

"Hrmph. Let me see." The manager opened a large ledger and ran a finger down the listings. "Ah yes. The Dodsons. They checked out about an hour ago. I can surely state that I was sorry to see them leave. Or at least, Mrs. Dodson. She was a most beautiful woman."

"Yeah. Thanks."

Spur walked out into the heavy, moist air. He couldn't believe that he'd spent an entire night in the room next to the thieves from Kansas City, and had spent the next morning in their bed.

"Really, Mr. Tompkins!" Clara Widdington said. "It was such a delight to meet you today." The aged woman fluttered her hands before her enormous bosom. "It's not often I get visitors from home. You could have sent me a telegram, after all."

"We left on such short notice," the gentleman

said.

"I see. I'm trying to remember when last I saw your parents. You hadn't been born then, of course; in fact, your mother and father had just met. When he came to me on that day in, oh when was it, 1840? 1845?"

"Something like that," he said, smiling.

Clara shook her head, sending her double chin bouncing. "Whenever it was. When your father called on me and told me that he was marrying some woman it broke my heart. Your father was always a ladies' man. I was so shocked to hear the news."

"People change."

The woman peered at him, nodded and smoothed her expensive silk dress over her knees. "Indeed they do. Would you care for some liquid refreshment, Edgar dear?"

"Yes. That would be lovely."

She smartly clapped her gloved hands. A black youth appeared.

"Yes, ma'am?"

"Jean, two mint juleps."

"Thank you, ma'am." The servant bowed and left.

As the elderly woman continued to talk of the "good old days," Lambert G. Hanover sat stiffly on the settee in Clara's parlor.

What a stroke of luck he'd had! Hanover had gone to a furniture store earlier that day, just to pass the time, and had fallen into talking with an obviously wealthy woman—his favorite kind. When he'd stated that he was from Philadelphia, she'd asked if he knew the Tompkins.

Indeed he did, Hanover had said, and told her that he was Edgar Tompkins, the couple's son. In fact, Hanover had worked for the Tompkins in their home right after running away from his parents. The woman had believed him and suddenly he was an accepted part of New Orleans high society.

It had been only too easy.

The servant appeared holding a silver tray. After Clara Widdington had selected her glass Hanover took his.

"A toast. To Philadelphia!" she said with a flourish.

They drank.

"Tell me. What is your new bride like?" she asked, dabbing the corners of her mouth with a lace handkerchief.

Hanover cleared his throat. "Well, she's beautiful, she's intelligent, a good dresser. She laughs at my jokes . . . ."

"Yes, yes, my dear. That much is obvious. But what about the really important things?" Clara's left eye twitched.

He took another sip and smiled. "Of course. Trust me. She comes from an impeccable background."

"Yes, yes. And?" The aged woman edged forward on her seat.

"And her parents are quite wealthy."

Mrs. Widdington touched her left hand to her bosom. "Thank goodness for that! I'd hate to think that you were breaking the family tradition, Edgar."

He smiled. "Are you sure it's no problem? Marie and I staying the night here? The steamship doesn't leave until five tomorrow afternoon."

"Of course it isn't any trouble!" Clara said, fluttering her left hand in front of her face. "It's kind of you to ask, but really, Edgar! Imagine you and Marie languishing in some classless hotel.

Besides, there isn't a room available in town. Something about some nonsensical steamboat race. I don't know." She set down her drink and patted his knee. "Besides, you're practically family. If things had turned out differently, I could be your mother, my dear."

He looked into her eyes. "That would have been lovely, Clara."

She raised the handkerchief to her nose.

Upstairs in Mrs. Widdington's home in New Orleans, Teresa went on an expedition. Lambert was keeping the woman occupied as she staked out exactly what they should take on their departure the next day.

There was so much jewelry that it dazzled Teresa's eyes. She couldn't resist slipping an emerald ring onto her finger. It fit perfectly. The ring held a huge, rectangular, nearly flawless emerald. It was so massive and so beautiful.

She placed the ring in her purse. The old biddy would never notice it being gone, and she certainly didn't have to tell Lamb about it.

Moving pictures and checking behind books, the beautiful woman finally found the safe. That was his strength, breaking into the confounded things, so she returned everything to its original appearance and memorized exactly which books the safe had been hidden behind.

That done, she returned to the room that the woman had given to Lamb and his "bride." She had to admit that the man was fabulous. It was so easy with him that she almost hated to leave New Orleans and board that cumbersome steamship tomorrow.

But he had to have his recreation as well, Teresa thought. He'd been complaining for two weeks now that all he really wanted to do was get back to the gambling that he loved so much. Starting tomorrow he'd have his chance.

Not just any card game satisfied Lambert G. Hanover, she thought wistfully as she checked her appearance in a gilt-framed mirror. It had to be very high stakes. The other players had to be of the highest social standing. He had to have thousands of dollars riding on the game or Lamb simply wasn't interested.

Certain that she looked fine, Teresa went downstairs.

"There are you, my dear!"

Hanover instantly stood and greeted her with a gentle kiss on her cheek.

"I hope you've found everything you need, my dear," Clara Widdington said.

"Oh, yes." She swung her purse. "Everything."

CHAPTER THIRTEEN

New Orleans. Teresa and Lambert G. Hanover. The three of them had gotten together, and the city by the Mississippi River had gathered its arms around them. Spur kicked over an empty milk can as he walked along Burgundy.

"Hey! Watch your fine steppin', sir!" a voice behind him said.

McCoy turned. A black woman stared at him from behind a half-opened door.

"I'm sorry." He tipped his hat and pulled at his sodden shirt. "This isn't the best day of my life."

She hooted. "You tellin' me?" The maid pushed the door fully open, revealing an elaborate garden in the courtyard and, behind it, a stately house. "Lordy, I'm overworked as it is. And now the missus invited some rich couple from out of town to stay the night." The round-faced woman tugged on her pristine uniform. "Midnight'll never come. That's when I head home. Just this morning the missus promised me I could leave early tonight and go bet on the Wheel of Fortune, instead of cookin' for three and lookin' after her unexpected guests.''

Spur nodded and began to walk away, but he turned back to her. The maid adjusted the white scarf she'd tied around her hair.

What if Teresa and Hanover hadn't gone to a different hotel? It wasn't likely that they'd leave New Orleans. Maybe they were staying with friends, or had managed to finagle their way into some wealthy household. It was an interesting idea.

"What're you staring at?" she asked.

"I'm sorry. Just thinking. You say that a rich couple came to call?" he asked.

She nodded. "Uh huh. White folks by the name of—oh, I can't think straight."

McCoy smiled and sat beside her on the stoop. The maid immediately rose.

"Sir! You shouldn't sit beside me. I know my station, and you should know yours! Fine thing it would be if anyone saw me putting on such high-faluting airs! It's against the natural order, me sitting beside you.''

He stood and took her arm. "My good woman, do you have a family?"

She nodded. "No husband, but yeah."

"What's your employer's name?"

"Miss Emily." She crossed her arms. "Why?"

A delivery cart rattled down the stone street.

"Could you tell me what Miss Emily's visitors look like?"

"And why should I do a thing like that?" she demanded.

Spur saw hope in her eyes. He reached into his coat pocket. "I could make it worth your time.''

The maid licked her lips. "Yeah?"

"What do they look like? These visitors from Pennsylvania?"

"Oh sir, I haven't seen much of them. Been in the kitchen all day long. Just used the front door to put out the milk can."

"But you got a glimpse?" Spur smiled and patted his pocket.

The maid's eyes ignited. "I may have." She delicately ran a hand down her chin and held it before her.

Spur proffered a silver dollar. The woman quickly grabbed it.

"Yes sir! I saw them all right. The woman—oh, she's a fine thing! Fancy dresses, hats that must've come from France. One of them could feed my family for a week." The maid bit the coin she'd just been paid. "And the gentleman!" She rolled her eyes.

"Is he tall? How old would you say they are?"

"Jasmine!" a female voice shrieked from inside the house far behind the maid.

"Coming, missy! Sir, I must go."

Spur gently took her arms. "Well?"

She looked at the house and then back at Spur. "Let the old biddy wait for her tea!" She arched her eyebrows at the forbidden thought. "Okay, sir. The gentleman's way shorter than you and round. He's as wide as he's tall! And the woman—his wife—why, she must be approachin' seven feet. A tall, gangling thing. But her dresses are so purty you don't notice at first."

"JASMINE!"

"Oh, I'm sorry, sir. I must be going. Please?"

Spur released her arms. "Thank you."

She disappeared behind the door. They certainly weren't the two he'd confronted in Wet Prong. It had seemed promising when she spoke of a fancy couple, but Spur should have known that it wouldn't be that easy to find two needles in the haystack of New Orleans.

He discovered a nearly hidden alley extending behind the fine house and plain doors that clearly marked the servants' entrances. Maybe Jasmine couldn't help him, but someone else might just have the clue that he needed.

He knocked at the first door, but the butler said that the master was out at the moment, and no; he'd had no guests.

The servants at the next house were of no help; their employers had gone to Paris. They'd left only a small caretaking staff behind them.

Another door, another knock. A shining-faced young girl giggled and said that her mother was having a baby and she had to run and boil some water.

Spur tried again and again, always coming up with nothing but determined to keep trying until he'd called at every fine house in the city.

As he lifted his fist to yet another back-street door, Spur knew that the con artists may have indeed gone to another hotel. But he doubted it. Why waste their time there when so many people were willing to put their valuables in danger at their hands?

"How will you explain it to Mrs. Widdington?" Lambert asked as he stared out the window in the room that their hostess had given them.

"Oh, something about how my hair started falling

out. She'll never suspect. Sometimes it helps to be a woman—other girls expect you to be vain." Teresa tugged and primped and fussed over her appearance in the full-length oval mirror until she was satisfied at the effect. "Well? What do you think? Do you like the wig?"

Lambert G. Hanover couldn't hide his astonishment. The woman before him wasn't Teresa Salvare. At least, it didn't look like her. The blonde hair was gone, covered with a dull red wig. A beauty mark was perfectly centered on her left cheek. Her lips, usually painted the brightest red, had softened to a less intense shade.

Most startlingly, his partner had somehow or another reduced the apparent size of her bust. Opening her eyes as wide as they'd go, Teresa tied on a bonnet and straightened her back.

"How do I look?" she sweetly asked.

His mouth opened.

"Don't stand there like a man who can't talk. What do you think?"

"My God," Lambert said. "Jesus. Teresa that's the most amazing transformation you've ever done!"

She laughed and held up her arms to display herself. "It's nothing for a woman of my temperament and rare theatrical abilities."

Lambert frowned. "I'm not sure how we'll explain you to Mrs. Widdington. Vanity aside, you look so different from the woman who walked in here that she's bound to notice. The old biddy might even get suspicious, and that wouldn't do either of us any good."

"Don't worry, Lamb. Mrs. Widdington's so old she can't think straight. Why, she must have introduced herself to me at least three times. And how often did she mention her beloved, long-haired cat?"

He roared. "That's right. The invisible cat that never seems to be around. It must've died years ago but she forgets it. Perhaps you're right, Teresa. Maybe she won't notice. But what if she does?"

Teresa smiled and sat on the embroidered, gilt chair. "If she does, I'm sure Mrs. Widdington's too much of a lady to mention it."

"Fine." He kissed her cheek. "The party begins at eight. We have to have everything packed before then."

"As usual," Teresa said with a sigh.

"You haven't forgotten the location of Mrs. Widdington's safe?"

"Of course not!" she haughtily said. "I know my job."

"Good."

"Just remember to tear yourself away from the gambling tables long enough to break into the old bag's safe. While I sit there and chat and do absolutely nothing."

"Tessa—" Lambert began.

She held up her hands. "I know. I know! It's best that way."

"I realize how boring it can be, pretending to be interested in gossip about persons you don't even know. But just one more night, my dear. That's all I ask."

She looked up at him. "Okay. But Lamb, just don't go back on your promise. After we sail on the *Natchez* up to St. Louis we will stop for a while. For all the money we've stolen we sure haven't been able to enjoy it! Why, we must have over $200,000, and just think of what we've had to do. Ride on horseback. Stay at filthy farmhouses. The dirt! The horrid food! The smell of horses!"

Hanover grinned. "My, you've become quite a lady. You weren't too refined when I dragged you out of that saloon! I've made you into a lady. A lady can put up with anything if she can increase her wealth. Be patient, my dear," Hanover said. He rubbed her shoulders. "In three or four days—depending upon how long the paddleboat race lasts—you'll be able to do anything you want. Anything!"

"Okay."

"What's the first thing you want to do?" He knelt beside her.

Teresa smiled. "Marry you."

"Be serious!"

"Okay. Buy everything I've ever wanted. Not dresses but things! Sparkling things. Shiny things!" Teresa looked at Lambert. "You're, ah, not going to lose all our money gambling, are you?"

"No, my dear. That I will not do."

"Sure." She sighed. "Of course not."

The young black boy rose from where he'd been kneeling. He hadn't been able to see anything through the keyhole, but the couple's voices had been easy to understand. They were criminals? They had stolen their money?

He walked down the second-story hall, avoiding stepping on those spots where the floorboards creaked. Why weren't they calling each other by the names that they'd given to Mrs. Widdington?

Jean scratched his head and went to the stairs. He didn't know what to make of all that he'd heard, but it certainly sounded like the man who'd come to stay at Mrs. Widdington's home wasn't Edgar

Tompkins from Pennsylvania.

They were thieves. Or least it seemed that way. Jean shook his head. Should he try to talk to the old woman? Warn her? He didn't know.

The only time he'd ever spoken more than one sentence to his employer had been when he'd shown up with a letter from one of her society friends pinned to his shirt saying that the son of one of her servants needed a job. She'd looked him over, sat him down in one of her fancy chairs and had a long talk with him.

Back then, Jean had been too young to be nervous. In the last two years Mrs. Widdington had barely noticed him unless she wanted something, such as one of her endless drinks. So they hadn't spoken again.

His daddy would know what to do, Jean thought. The boy rubbed his eyes and went downstairs. His fourteen-year-old mind couldn't settle on an answer.

Tell her, he thought.

No, don't tell her. What's she to you?

She pays me good money.

No, not enough money.

Tell her right now.

Don't tell her!

Jean sighed and straightened his white coat. He went into the parlor.

Mrs. Widdington glanced up at him.

"Oh, Jean, you startled me! I was just studying the Psalms. What is it?" she pleasantly asked.

He couldn't talk.

"Now really, Jean?" Mrs. Widdington laughed and twirled her reading glasses in her left hand. "Don't be nervous. You know you can speak to me."

He violently wrung his hands before him. "Yes,

Mrs. Widdington. But. . . ."

The wealthy woman set down her Bible. "Just say it, my dear boy."

Jean swallowed. "Uh, your guests, miss."

"What about them?"

"I was going up to put the flowers in your room and I—I heard them—"

Mrs. Widdington leaned closer. Her eyes narrowed on either side of her hawklike nose. "Yes? What did you hear them doing?"

He blushed.

"I know you don't speak much. At least, you never have around me. Some folks might think you were afraid of me. But Jean, if you have something to say then simply tell me! What is it?"

"Are you sure he's who he says he is?"

She went blank. "Jean, whatever are you talking about? Of course he's Edgar Tompkins!"

"Yes ma'am. But—but they were talkin' about stealin' and thievery and all that."

Mrs. Widdington molded her face into a smile. "I believe I told you not to listen in at doors, Jean. You simply misunderstood them. Edgar and Marie were probably discussing some problem they had in the past with thieves. I'm afraid it's rather common among some servants."

"Ah—ah—"

"No need to worry." She propped the glasses on her nose and picked up her Bible.

"Yes ma'am. Thank you, ma'am."

Jean's knees shook as he walked from the parlor. He'd known she wouldn't believe him. But he had heard them—the woman saying they'd robbed a lot of money. Calling each other by different names. And her going on about some wig.

Jean stopped at the kitchen door. The young black boy turned around, searched the empty house behind him with his eyes and walked through the double doors. The fragrance of simmering soup lulled him into forgetting everything but getting a mouthful of supper before it was laid on the rustic table.

Dusk sank onto the city. Spur pushed into a dark alley. The feeble light from kerosene lanterns had already begun to shine in a few windows. Just a couple more houses and he'd stop that part of his investigation.

A cat cried out and shot past him. McCoy grinned and moved deeper into the alley. The houses weren't so fancy now. The neighborhood wasn't as good.

The alleyway turned inky. Somewhere in the distance he heard feet rustle. Probably some servant hurrying home with the master's whiskey, he thought.

There was no answer at the first door. He walked to the next. It was difficult to decide where to place his feet; he couldn't see the cobblestone surface of the alley in the darkness. Half by feel and half by insight, Spur made his way to the next house.

His knock brought a startled, elderly white woman who clutched a kerosene lamp to the door. Her lined face peered at him from behind the door.

"What are you doing out there? White folks call at the front!"

"I'm looking for a couple." Spur had said it so many times that the words flowed out. He was surprised to see the woman. She wasn't dressed as a servant.

"I don't know about any rich man and woman!"

she said. "But since you're out there, have you seen my wild-eyed slave—I mean, serving girl?"

Spur winced at the woman's slip. Apparently, she was one of the many who hadn't accepted the fact that, in the United States, human beings could no longer own other human beings. "Sorry, no ma'am."

She curled her upper lip. "It figures. That bitch snuck out around half-past six. Probably to see that good-for-nothing boyfriend of hers. Lord only knows what they're doing out there in the dark."

"No one out here but me," Spur said. "At least I haven't seen anyone."

The woman frowned. "I've got ten guests for a sit-down dinner and no one to serve them! I'm sure that boy's master'll track them down and beat his hide."

"Thanks for your help, ma'am." Spur sighed as the door closed, cutting off the slice of light.

Just two more houses, he told himself. Then he could quit and get a well-deserved drink.

Voices ahead. A man and a woman laughing. Someone else silenced them with a low "shush!" A drum softly sounded under an unseen player's hand.

The alley was so dark that he couldn't see a blessed thing. Curious, Spur walked deeper into it. Something glinted about ten yards ahead. Metal? A weapon?

He couldn't tell, but it sounded like a party was beginning right there in the alley. A woman began singing in a language which McCoy had never before heard. More laughter. Objects clinked together. Feet shuffled on the paved surface of the alley.

He fought the impulse to call out to them. This

might get interesting, he thought. If nothing else it would break the monotony of the day. Spur stealthily approached them, making no sound.

A circle of light blazed into existence. The match moved and created another flame. Then two more sprang from the darkness and danced. The three candles barely illuminated the wizened black woman's face. Spur saw chicken feathers fly in the breeze that had kicked up as the sun set.

"When we get through with this, old man Franklin'll never beat you again, Lyle!" a wizened old woman said. "Your master is done gonna have the gris-gris put on him."

Spur's fascination with the strange spectable before him didn't prevent him from hearing the footsteps rapidly approaching from behind.

Someone was coming.

The candles flared. The drumming went on. Wary of being attacked, Spur darted through the darkness across the broad alley. Just as he made it to the wall explosions shattered the nighttime air with light and thundering sounds.

CHAPTER FOURTEEN

A man screamed in the pitch-dark alley. The candle flames were quickly pinched out. Boots hit the cobblestones. Spur flattened against the far wall and jerked his head back and forth, trying to figure out what was going on without becoming too involved.

"I got you now, Lyle!" a man's voice said. "Git on up here and there'll be no trouble! You know you aren't supposed to leave without my permission!"

"No!"

A grunt. "I figured you'd be out tomcattin' with your woman. Then I find out you're voodooin'! Get your black ass back into the house, Forder. Now!"

Spur couldn't resist. "Slavery was abolished years ago," he said.

"Who was that? Who said that? Damn, it's so dark in here. Johnny, hand me that lantern."

Seconds later Spur heard liquid sloshing onto the ground. A match roared into life. It quickly lit the kerosene, transforming the inky alley into a brightly lit corner of New Orleans. McCoy drew his Colt.

A portly man in an expensive suit chomped on the end of his cigar and trained his pistol down the alley. Behind him stood a younger man with the same face. Probably his son, Spur thought. On the other side of him, up against the dead end of the alley, stood three blacks: a young couple and the elderly woman he'd seen earlier.

"Back away from here!" McCoy shouted as the kerosene flamed before him.

"You protecting my boy?" the fat man asked.

"You're treating him like a slave. He isn't your property. He's a human being."

The Southerner guffawed. "Says you. Forder, I'm giving you ten seconds to be by my side. If you don't move I'll shoot your girlfriend. Then I'll shoot your mother. If that doesn't convince you, well, boy, I'll shoot you. Come here!"

"Leave us alone!" the servant yelled. The two woman screamed.

"I'm warning you. Go home!" Spur shouted.

The man altered his aim. "I'm getting powerfully tired of your yakking," he said. "Maybe I'll just take care of you first!"

"Try it."

Spur drew and peeled off a shot. Before the man could react the bullet had sent his weapon spinning from his hand. McCoy smiled at the surprising accuracy of his aim, especially considering that he only had the dancing light of the fire in the street to work with.

"Sumbitch! You nearly shot my head off!" The obese Southerner turned to his son. "Johnny! Give me your—"

Spur fired again. The bullet passed between Johnny's legs and dug into a plaster wall just behind him.

"Drop it," McCoy said.

"Shit, boss!" The weapon fell to the ground.

"Thanks. Now, Johnny, I suggest you and that over-fed slaveowner get your butts out of this alley before I decide to start shooting at something else!"

"You can't do this, Yankee!"

Spur waved with his weapon. "Willing to bet your worthless life on that? Get moving!"

The well-dressed Southerner shook his head. "I'll be back for you, Fordor!" he yelled as he and Johnny disappeared around the corner.

"Everyone all right?" Spur yelled toward the rear of the alley before he looked away from the now deserted alley entrance.

Silence. He turned and saw that the three of them had gone. Disappeared.

A quick check of the area showed no blood. He hoped no one had been hurt. Spur sighed, waited until the kerosene had harmlessly burned itself out and chose a new alley. He had to find Teresa and Hanover.

Mrs. Widdington placed her Bible on her lap. She didn't believe Jean for an instant. The boy was becoming quite uncontrollable. First it had been his sudden interest in girls. And now this! Accusing her houseguests of being thieves!

She shook her head and climbed the stairs. Edgar and his bride were apparently still preparing for her party that evening. Light shone from under their door. Clara Widdington smiled as she thought of those far-off days in which she'd dreamed of marrying that other Tompkins, the man who'd swept into her life and breezed out almost as quickly as he'd come.

The woman turned up the kerosene lamp in her bedroom and sat before the mirror. Now, what to wear? Clara smiled and tapped her chin. Of course; the green silk that she'd already decided on. How silly of her to forget. But what to go with it?

She lifted the wooden lid of her jewelry box. Definitely not the rubies. Sapphires wouldn't do either, and she feared that the diamond pendant would seem too ostentatious. The emerald ring would be fine.

Clara Widdington searched through the box. When she couldn't find it, she sighed and went through a second tangled collection. As she rummaged through gold bracelets, strands of perfectly matched pearls and other mementoes of past suitors, Clara remembered how she'd happened to receive the emerald ring.

The fine English Duke had been so admiring of her charms that after—what was it, two or three nights together?—he'd gone out and purchased the ring for her. That was some time ago and she'd rarely worn it since.

But tonight she had to have it. After five minutes of searching Clark Widdington realized that it wasn't there.

She felt her heartbeat rise in her agitation. Calm yourself, she said, fanning her face. Jean had mentioned thieves. Clara smiled. Of course! The boy had taken a fancy to some new girl and had to have extra money to spend on her. He'd stolen her ring!

* * *

Teresa lowered her voice. "I just have a feeling, Lamb. We can't go to that party tonight."

Hanover allowed himself a grunt. "You just don't want me to have any fun. You're afraid I'll bankrupt us gambling."

"No, that's not it at all." She tugged at her wig. "Something's up. I can't be sure what it is, but all is not right here."

"That sounds like a line from one of your plays." Hanover lit a cigar and contentedly puffed. "My dear, the race doesn't start until 5:04 P.M. tomorrow. Why leave now before the party, before I can have the chance to legally earn some spending money?"

"Legally?" Teresa laughed. "You're the crookedest player I've ever seen. Shaving your cards. Weighting your dice. I know all about it, Lambert!"

He stood. "Tessa, that's a lie. I never cheat! Well, at least not at cards. Besides a—"

"A gentleman wouldn't cheat. Ha! Lamb, don't change the subject. I don't care. You can gamble somewhere else, anywhere else in town but here!"

"Lower your voice!" He stubbed out his cigar. "I don't understand why you're so nervous, Tessa. This isn't like you at all. Is it because of that lawman? The one you took into our bed? The one you made love to?"

She flung herself onto the bed. "Maybe it is. I don't know. Call it woman's intuition. I can distract her for five or ten minutes. You can get into the safe. Why, she might have more money than we can carry!"

"Unless she puts it in a bank." Hanover crossed his arms and studied the woman who sat on the bed and looked brightly at him.

"As soon as we're settled into a hotel, I promise you we'll be so busy in our room we won't have time to sleep."

Hanover began to speak.

"That is, after you've gambled as much as you want." She rushed through the soothing words.

"Well . . . ."

"It wouldn't do for you to be rusty on the steamer. What do you think?"

He sighed. "Okay. Fine! Gentlemen don't argue with women if they can possible avoid it. Get packed. I'll take a look. Then keep the woman and that nosy servant of hers out of the way for at least fifteen minutes. With my luck she's got a safe that's hard to break into."

Spur called at three more houses but the servants were too busy to talk to him for more than a few seconds. They shooed him away as soon as they saw that he wasn't a friend or a late deliveryman.

Frustrated and still angry at having allowed himself to be tricked by the beautiful criminal he'd been following, McCoy walked out onto Basin Street. Garish music blasted from the rows of saloons and gambling "palaces" that lined both sides of the narrow avenue. Glamorous women, unfettered by the conventions and dangers of the west, strolled unaccompanied, looking for customers.

"How about it, honey?" a delicious belle asked as he walked by.

"Sorry. I like horses."

Spur heard her laughing as drunks made their nightly rounds, prostitutes perched against walls and fistfights broke out around him. He had to get to just a few more houses.

McCoy had nowhere else to look.

An imposing, magnificent house came into view as he turned a corner. He checked the back of the building but there was no rear entrance. Spur straightened his hat and walked up to the front.

A very young black boy opened the door and gazed up at him.

"You here for the party?" he asked.

"What?"

"You here for the party?"

"Ah, no."

"Sorry." The uniformed servant started closing the door.

"Wait! I'm looking for a pair of thieves. Well-dressed, elegant white folks. In their thirties. The woman's tall and blonde."

The boy's mouth dropped. "That's them!"

"I'm a lawman. You won't get into any trouble. Know anything about them?"

He looked back into the house and nodded. "Mrs. Widdington didn't believe me! But it's true! They said they'd stolen all kinds of money."

"Jean! You little devil!" a woman said from inside the house. "Where's my emerald ring? If you stole it I'll forgive you, but not until you give it back to me."

Spur's gaze met the boy's eyes. The kid shook with fear.

No time to waste. McCoy pushed open the door and rushed into the well-furnished house.

A large woman was hurrying down the stairs. Her fleshy face was a mask of anger.

"What are you doing here?" she demanded as she

reached the floor. "And where's Jean? Have you seen my houseboy?"

Spur twisted around and saw the empty doorway. He didn't blame the kid for running away.

"No, ma'am." He tipped his hat. "You're missing an emerald ring?"

"Darn tooting!" she said. "I just checked. It isn't in the box I've kept it in for, oh, fifteen years."

"Who are you?"

"Mrs. Clara Widdington."

"And you have houseguests?"

She drew back. "Why yes."

"They stole it. I'm with the Secret Service. Name's Spur McCoy."

"Secret Service? Why, I knew a man once—"

"Where are they?"

"Who?"

"Your houseguests, Mrs. Widdington?" McCoy shouted.

"Why, upstairs, but—"

He ran to them and flew to the landing. Once there he checked every door along the hall. The first revealed an empty, long-disused room. The second was obviously a guest room. Luggage was piled in every corner. Fancy dresses laid in heaps.

And the window was open.

CHAPTER FIFTEEN

Spur ran to the opened window and leaned through the frame. The street below was deserted, but just below the window grew a massive gardenia bush. The seven-foot-tall shrub could have broken the thieves' fall as they escaped.

"Sir, I must ask you what you're doing in my house!" Clara Widdington said as she stepped into the room.

Spur turned back to her. "Your guests seem to have left."

"Really? Impossible! I've been in the parlor since early this afternoon. The front door is the only exit from this house. I would have seen them walk by."

He shook his head. "She was blonde? Beautiful? And he was a rich, thin, tall gentleman?"

"Yes, that's them," the dowager said.

"Great!" He pushed a foot through the windowsill.

"Sir, I don't know what's going on here! Things

are entirely out of control!"

"Your houseboy didn't steal your emerald ring,"
Spur said as he stuck his left foot outside as well.
"It was Lambert G. Hanover and his lady."

"*The* thieves from Kansas City?" Mrs.
Widdington said. "Friends told me about them!"

"Yeah. Nice meeting you."

He bent over double. When his torso was free of
the window frame, Spur stared at a distant light
and pushed off.

The gardenia bush cushioned his body as he fell
the eight feet from the window. Spur jumped to the
ground, brushed off his clothes and stooped to
retrieve his hat. There, beside the fragrant tree, lay
a ten dollar bill.

They had come that way! But where had they
gone? No one was in sight, save for a few children
and their weary mother who trotted after them
down the street.

Spur lit a match. He clearly saw the impressions
of a man's and woman's footwear in the moist, bare
earth. They headed away from the house and out
onto Duphine Street.

"At least I've been robbed by the best!" Mrs. Widdington yelled from the house as McCoy set off to
follow the pair's tracks.

It was easy at first. He kept stopping and
checking by the light of matches to ensure that he
was still on their path. From the looks of the deep,
somewhat abbreviated footprints, their boots
hadn't lingered in their endless contacts with the
ground. The pair had been running.

The piles of clothing in their room clearly
indicated that Teresa and Hanover hadn't taken
anything but money with them. If they hadn't left

it at some location between New Orleans and Kansas City, that is. They were traveling light and on foot, but unless Teresa was a tougher woman than Spur thought she was, they'd have to rest. At least one of them would have to.

Where would they go? Spur wondered. To a hotel. That would be the obvious choice. Then, first thing tomorrow, they'd buy a brand-new set of belongings and clothing and go on with their dirty work.

He struck a lucifer on a stone and sneered at the sight. The footprints he'd been following were lost in the wake of a carriage that must have passed by only moments before. A few feet further and the unpaved street was covered with hundreds of footprints of every kind. Hanover and Teresa had effectively covered their trail.

McCoy cursed as the match burnt his thumb. He shook his head. Go to the first hotel, he told himself. They had to find a place to spend the night.

"It's all your fault!" Teresa said as she hung the bags containing their money on the wall of the horse stall.

"All my fault? Woman, I agree with you. I was just going down to the safe when we heard the old biddy yelling about her emerald ring. Five seconds later you've grabbed the cash and we're flying out the window! And I got a hole in my best suit."

"What does that matter? By morning your gentleman's clothes will be covered with horse shit!"

"Tessa!" Hanover said.

"I said shit and I meant shit! Not dung, not manure, but shit!"

Hanover sighed and leaned against the empty stable. "Honestly, Teresa! Such language!"

"Don't get so uppity with me!" she said, brushing away the soiled straw in search of the clean. "You've said it often enough."

"That's right, my sweet. And it's all I've been hearing from you lately."

They'd been lucky enough to find an empty livery stable and had walked right in.

"Just admit it," she asked.

"Admit what?"

"Oh come on, Lamb! I didn't exactly have to force you out of that window. You recognized his voice, too. That man who was talking to Mrs. Widdington." Teresa gave up on her guest and sat on the fragrant straw.

"Yes. It was that lawman from Wet Prong."

"His name's Spur McCoy. I told you that."

"I don't know how he did it, but he found us."

"He was just lucky. That's all." She leaned against the open boards that created the stall and wrinkled her nose.

"No. He's very good."

"Don't tell me you're worried about him? After all the lawman we've had chasing us?" Teresa softly laughed. "I'm worrying about you, Lamb."

He turned to her from across the stall. "Why couldn't you control yourself, Tessa? Taking that ring was the stupidest thing you've ever done."

She nodded. "I know. But it was pretty. I never thought she'd miss it."

"And because of it we're out an untold sum of money."

Teresa stood, unhooked her purse from the wall and rummaged inside it. Seconds later she sat again and held her hand toward Hanover.

Even in the darkness, he whistled at the sparkle

and flash of green fire within the stone.

"Isn't it a beauty?" she asked.

"I have to say that it is," Hanover rose to his knees and moved closer to her. He took Teresa's hand in his. "It's the largest emerald I've ever seen."

"But worthless for resale, right?"

"Yes. Too risky." He swiftly removed the ring from the woman's finger and threw it into the next stable.

"Hey! Lambert G. Hanover, are you out of your mind?" She scrambled to stand on the slippery straw.

"Stay right there, woman!"

In her anger and surprise, Teresa stumbled to her feet and stood.

The man grabbed her wrist and threw her onto the ground. Her body bounced on the lush straw. Standing over her, Hanover pointed at her lovely face.

"You will go to sleep. You will not look for that ring. You'll leave it behind here to remind yourself of how dangerous your frivolous ways can be."

"But—"

"No. Shut up. Good night."

Lambert laid beside her and placed an arm around her body. She sniffled and finally relaxed into the stinking but fairly comfortable straw.

"At least we still have the money, Lamb. At least we still have that."

"Yes. And each other."

Spur had followed a dozen false trails, trying to find one that led directly to one of the big hotels that were only a few streets away. But each time he'd soon realized that he'd been fooling himself.

Asking at the desks for them would be meaningless. They would never use their correct names. What could he do? Check every single room in every single hotel in the town of New Orleans?

Spur pounded his fist into his left hand. Might as well turn in for the night and start again in the morning. More out of habit than anything else, he lit his last match and bent down to inspect the ground.

Surprisingly, the area was fairly clear. He saw a familiar set of boot impressions that were remarkably similar to the ones that had led away from Mrs. Widdington's house. Dragging from exhaustion and an unsatisfied appetite, Spur wearily followed the tracks.

A man and a woman had walked this way recently. That was certain. But who was it? Hanover and Teresa, or some other couple?

He'd followed them for 50 feet before the match burned out. Spur got down on his hands and knees. He almost smiled as the tracks were lost in a sea of fresh horseshoe impressions. It made sense. He was near a livery stable.

He stretched, yawned and walked to the small barn that lay to the rear of the workshed. Peering in through a hole between two timbers, Spur saw nothing but a succession of empty stalls and dimly-lit heaps of straw.

No one was there.

The next morning, Spur rose, gave himself a whore's bath and shaved. Dressed in fresh clothing, he went down to the restaurant for some breakfast.

It was jammed. Men, women and children were practically dancing on their toes. Spur pushed

through them and finally made it inside the
restaurant, but no food was in sight on the tables.
Instead, a bearded, black-coated man was
addressing the crowd.

"And I, Captain Thomas Leathers of the steamer
Natchez, can assure you fine folks that I and my
vessel are not involved in any race with any other
boat that may leave New Orleans this day."

Raucous laughter echoed throughout the
restaurant.

"Sure, Leathers," a distinguished man said.
"Neither am I."

An elderly man holding fistfuls of dollars strode
up and stood between the two men. "Really?" he
said. "Then tell me something, Captain Cannon.
How come the *Robert E. Lee* is leaving today at 5:00
with no cargo? No passengers? And no earthly
reason for sailing to St. Louis?"

"I already told you, Posner. I'm sailing the *Lee*
to Louisville to pick up a shipment. It is Captain
Leathers that is racing today—not I."

The laughter pounded in Spur's head.

"You mealy-mouthed, egg-sucking old fart!"
Leathers said. "I'm doing no such thing!"

John Cannon fingered his long white beard and
smiled. "And neither am I."

Uproarious laughter. Money changed hands all
around Spur. A momentous race was about to begin
—despite the men's assurances to the contrary—
and everyone was betting on it.

He vaguely recalled hearing about it and seeing
posters concerning the race when he got into town.
Spur scratched his stomach and realized he'd get
no food in that restaurant. When a fresh mass of
people pushed against him, trying to squeeze into

the already crowded room, Spur slipped through them and went outside.

He stopped as the sunlight hit him. A race. The couple in the hotel room next to his had mentioned a race two nights ago. That had been Teresa and Hanover.

He made a mental note. If he didn't catch up with them by 4:00 that afternoon, he'd be watching a race between two steamships—the *Natchez* and the *Robert E. Lee.*

CHAPTER SIXTEEN

Teresa Salvare dipped sparkling water into her hands and poured it over her body. Around her, the world awoke. Birds sang. Clouds passed far overhead. The stream trickled. And sunlight flooded the cottonwood and willow trees that hid her bath from prying eyes.

She could only smile as she cleansed her body of the effects of her night in a dirty horse stall. How ridiculous! They had more money than they could spend in a year and yet they couldn't do any better than an empty livery stable for lodgings. It was absurd, but true.

Enough of this bathing, she thought, and wriggled her perfectly formed nude body. The filtered sunlight and a gentle breeze both warmed and chilled her. As she looked up onto the bank of the nameless stream, Teresa realized that if Lamb didn't return soon she'd be trapped in the open, naked, with nowhere to go.

Footsteps crunched through the underbrush ahead. She instinctively bent and hid behind a stand of brilliant orange and black coneflowers.

"Tessa?" a man's voice softly said.

Lambert appeared with two sets of clothing over his arms.

She stood and ran to him. "I thought you'd never get here! Figured you might've run off with some woman."

He arched his eyebrows and laid the woman's clothing over a bush. "Aren't you forgetting, my dear? All the money's back here with you. I'm not that stupid. Now hurry and dress while I have my bath."

"Okay. Did you have any trouble getting the clothing?" Teresa said, bending to study the florid red silk dress.

Lambert G. Hanover undressed. "Not at all. I found a very accommodating woman who sympathized with our plight—being thrown from our carriage—and she was so glad to help out."

"How sweet! Get into that water, Lamb. You smell like you spent the night in horse dung!"

"Dung?"

Teresa struggled into the single petticoat her partner had managed to get. "Yes. This morning, it's dung."

After breakfast, Spur found the front page of a newspaper in the road. It had been ground into the dirt but was still readable. Dated Thursday, June 30, which was today's date, it wouldn't have caught his eye if it hadn't had a screaming headline:

THE STEAMERS WILL RACE!!
Despite their claims to the contrary, Captain

John W. Cannon of the *Robert E. Lee* and Captain Thomas P. Leathers of the *Natchez* will indeed launch their momentous race at exactly 5 o'clock this afternoon. Cannon has stripped his vessel of all cargo and even passengers to increase his speed, while Leathers is taking both on board as usual.

Enquiries have been coming in from San Francisco, New York, St. Louis, London, Lisbon, Paris and many other cities. The worldwide attention which has been drawn to the race has undoubtedly caused millions of dollars to be bet on the outcome. We'll know in three or four days who will come out ahead. The stakes are, of course, high: The captain who proves that his steamer is the fastest during the 1,200 mile race will undoubtedly enjoy the most cotton shipping business in the future.

This is the race of the century! The Mississippi will become a gigantic raceway for the two captains, well-known within town for their mutual dislike. The *Picayune* will produce a special race issue with all the results as soon as they're known.

McCoy reread the article. Millions of dollars have been bet? Hmmm. Were Hanover and Teresa planning on stealing that money, or perhaps the funds of the passengers which, according to the article, will only be riding on the *Natchez?*

Spur walked down to the wharf. Dozens of boats of every description bobbed gently on the slow-moving water. He saw the *Princess,* the *Dubuque, City of Chester* and several other before he finally spotted both the *Natchez* and the *Robert E. Lee.* The names of the last two had been proudly repainted over the sternwheels.

The *Robert E. Lee* was unusually quiet for a working steamer. No roustabouts were loading bales of cotton. No early arriving passengers were waiting to go on board. The ship was practically deserted. Even the boiler deck was empty of its usually boisterous hands.

The *Natchez*, however, gave the appearance of businss as usual. Spur watched the sturdy-boiled, black men hauling cotton on board. Off-duty deck hands crouched in circles, probably enjoying a round of that dice game they'd invented—craps.

The air filled with the smell of wood smoke. A riverboat slipped its moorings. White steam and smoke poured from the two sets of stacks. The *Dubuque* majestically moved upriver, joining the ragtag fleet of barges, rafts and keelboats that littered the surface of the Mississippi River.

As he watched the *Dubuque* head away from New Orleans, Spur felt all of his efforts toward capturing Hanover and Teresa flowing away as well.

But he still had at least one chance of finding them before the *Natchez* left on "the race of the century." The thieves had left Mrs. Widdington's house without their luggage. If they were going to pass themselves off as rich folks, they'd have to get new clothes.

Spur sighed and headed for the dress and fine men's wear stores. Every single one of them was closed, so he went to a saloon, stood at the bar and got a watered whiskey.

He drank, listened in on the local gossip, played one hand of poker and returned to his hotel. As he walked in the deskman called him over.

"Good morning, sir. A telegram came in for you just a few moments ago."

He took the wire and went up to his room. Sitting on his bed, Spur ripped open the envelope and read the message.

It was to the point. General Halleck wanted to know how he was doing on the case and when he'd be turning over Lambert G. Hanover and Teresa Salvare to the proper authorities—alive, if at all possible. He was also instructed to recover as much of the money, stocks and bonds as he could find.

Spur crumpled the telegram and threw it against the far wall of his hotel room. So her last name was Salvare. That was news to him, he thought, as he took off his hat and stretched out on the bed. McCoy crossed his legs and wedged his hands behind his head. This was the worst case he'd ever worked on.

Absolutely no leads. Nothing to go on. Spur closed his eyes, hoping it would help him think.

A vigorous knocking on the door roused him from his mental activity. He rose and went to it. The lovely face shocked and surprised him.

"Good, you're here, Mr. McCoy," the blonde-haired woman said. "May I come in?"

He smiled and stepped back to allow Teresa Salvare into his hotel room. He should march her to the police but she was only half the prize he was after. He'd play along for as long as possible.

"How've you been, Marie?"

Teresa twirled her white parasol. "As well as can be expected. I was, ah, staying at a friend's house but she up and died. I mean, the poor dear *dropped dead* before my very eyes!" She laid on a smooth Southern accent. "It was so horrifying that I didn't know what to do."

"And so you came to me for comfort?"

Teresa looked back into the hall. "Well, not exactly. You see, I didn't tell you much about myself yesterday, after we—well, you know." She smiled.

"No?"

"No. In fact, I didn't tell you anything."

Spur started to close the door. Teresa went to it.

"Ah, leave it open!" she cried.

"Open?" He sighed. "I guess you didn't come back here for round three."

"No." The parasol spun in an endless circle. "You see, I'm—I'm in trouble."

He nodded. Was she actually willing to confess? It didn't seem possible that this was the woman who'd threatened to kill him in Wet Prong, and had most probably tried to do so in her hotel room.

"What kind of trouble?"

Teresa closed her umbrella and rested its tip on the floor. "I—I don't know how to tell you this."

"Just go ahead. It's best to get things out in the open. Don't you think?"

She smiled. "That's just what my mother always used to say. Okay. The truth is, I find that I'm rather, ah, low on funds. When I saw the dress shops here I spent and spent. Then there were the hotel feels and dining and—well, Spur, I'm flat broke. I don't have a penny to my name."

He tried to look sympathetic. "Poor woman!" Spur had to admire her: she was an excellent actress. No wonder Teresa and Hanover had been such successful con artists. "What can I do for you?"

She paced and looked around the room. "Well, ah, if you would find it in your heart to make me a small loan, I would make it worth your while."

Teresa Salvare stopped and gazed at him. She parted her lips and smiled. "I truly would. And I'd repay you as soon as I could."

"Well, it won't do, a beautiful woman like you in this city short on funds." What was she getting at? Had she and Hanover left the money somewhere on the way to New Orleans? Or had she hardened herself and was about to kill him? But if the latter was the case, why hadn't she let him close the door? Nothing made any sense.

"Of course, Marie. All you had to do was to ask." He reached into his pockets, frowned and snapped his fingers. "Damn! I just deposited most of my money in a local bank. Can't be too careful with all the pickpockets around here."

She smiled. "Of course."

"I could write you a check—"

"I would appreciate it, but what I really need is cash. You see, I'm supposed to be leaving on a riverboat this afternoon and I can't pay for my passage."

"Hmmmm." Spur pretended to think it over. "Tell you what. Let's run down to the bank. I could withdraw as much as you need. Then, when you're back on your feet again, you could send the money to my uncle, General Halleck, in Washington, D.C."

"Your uncle is a general?" she asked, still playing the Southern belle.

"Now now, Marie. No sense in worrying over the war. Besides, he never went into the field."

"I'm sure. That would be absolutely wonderful, Spur!" She kissed his cheek. "That way I could leave New Orleans and get back home!" Her eyes shined.

He walked to the bed and picked up his hat.

"Where is home, Marie? Where do you live?"

"Well, I'm originally from Baton Rouge, but I'm rejoining my brother and his young ones in St. Louis. His wife left him just a few months ago and the poor dear simply can't take care of everything alone."

Time to get things moving. "I see." He straightened the wide-brim Stetson on his head and grunted. "Shall we go now, *Teresa*?"

"Yes. I can't thank you enough—" Her eyes widened. "My name's Marie."

"Sure it is. Where's Hanover?"

Their gazes met.

"I don't know what you're talking about."

"You can drop the Southern accent, Teresa. If you won't talk I guess I'll have to lock you up by yourself. He'll come after you." Spur pointed toward the hall. "Now walk!"

"Just like that?" Teresa asked.

"Yes. You came here to confess, didn't you?"

"No. That's not what I came here for at all." Teresa moved to the door.

Spur closely followed her. Just as she stepped out of the room, she dropped her parasol and put a hand to her mouth.

"Oh dear! I almost forgot something!"

"What's that?" Spur asked.

Teresa Salvare ripped the bodice of her dress and screamed as loud as she could.

"RAPE!"

CHAPTER SEVENTEEN

"What are you talking about?" Spur McCoy demanded as he stood outside his hotel room.

"Rape! Rape!"

Teresa Salvare grabbed Spur's hands and immediately pretended to wrestle herself from his grasp. Her dress and petticoats flailing around her, the woman pushed her way through the doorway and ran out into the hall, gasping, crying hysterically.

Two burly men at the end of the hall rushed up to her. Both wore uniforms.

"Hotel security, ma'am," one of them said, frowning below his thick red moustache. "What seems to be the problem?"

"He—he tried to rape me!" Teresa said. Catching her breath, she started to scream again. "He tried to pull my dress right off of me!"

Spur stood his ground. "This is outrageous! I did no such thing. She's lying!" Spur said.

One of the security guards raised an eyebrow. "Uh huh. And I suppose she ripped her dress all by herself, right? With no help from you?"

"Precisely."

Teresa increased the volume of her screams, stopping only to yell. "He said he'd kill me if I didn't—didn't—"

McCoy couldn't believe what was happening. The woman had set him up. She'd planned the whole thing. That was why she hadn't allowed him to close the door.

"Come with us, sir," the red-haired security guard said. "Help me out, Burroughs."

The two men warily advanced on Spur and quickly grabbed his arms. He was immobile. The woman's sudden actions had confused him to the point that he hadn't drawn his weapon.

"Take him away!" Teresa screeched. "Lock him up! Such vicious men shouldn't be allowed to walk the streets of New Orleans! I hate this city! I hate all men! The nerve of him thinking he could compromise my virtue!"

"Gentlemen!" Spur shouted above the woman's raucous voice. "I'm Spur McCoy, an agent of the United States Secret Service. This woman is wanted for robbery in Kansas city and right here in this town. She's trying to—"

The men tightened their grip.

"Unhand me!"

"Shut up!"

The pair of burly hotel security guards rustled Spur to the stairs and "helped" him down them. Heads turns as the three men walked across the lobby. Spur regained his senses and didn't struggle as they stepped into the sunshine.

"Sergeant Malbrough!" Burroughs said as a big-headed man barrelled down the street toward them.

"What is it, Don? Some trouble at the hotel again?"

"A woman complained that this man just tried to rape her. Right in the Hollister."

"Good work, men," the police sergeant said as he removed Spur's Colt .45 from his holster. "Would you be so kind as to escort him to the jail? He's a big 'un. I think I'll need your help."

"Be glad to, sir. Come on!"

"Sergeant Malbrough, this is uncalled for!" Spur yelled. "The woman who said I attacked her is wanted for robbery in at least two states, possibly more. If you'll send a telegram to General Halleck in Washington, at the Secret Service, I'm sure we can clear all this up."

"Oh, of course we can," he said, beaming. "Of course we can!" He went to speak with Teresa Salvare, who stood sobbing in the middle of the street.

Twenty minutes later, Spur was behind bars. He hadn't tried to resist because he was weaponless and outnumbered. Now, as he sat in the filthy, damp jail cell, Spur stared at the green fungus that grew along the walls and sighed.

The woman was absolute poison. She was so audacious, waltzing into his room and then charging him with rape just to get him out of the way for a while. Though the charges wouldn't stick, it could prevent him from stopping Teresa and Hanover from boarding the *Natchez* before its historic trip to St. Louis. If the racing boat was as fast as the paper had said, it would be there in record time and he'd be still rotting in a New

Orleans jail cell.

Even if he was suddenly released just moments after the *Natchez* sailed it would take him weeks to ride up to St. Louis. Hanover and Teresa would have vanished by then, with the money they'd stolen, and he would be suffering through the humiliation of his first failure at solving a case since he'd started working for the Secret Service.

The thought made him grunt. McCoy stood and paced the 8 foot by 7 foot room. He hadn't seen anyone since he'd been dumped into the cell. The sergeant had had to go off to do something and no one else was around. Even the other cells were empty, save for two snoring drunkards who shared one among them. They lay face down on the floor.

Spur grabbed a tin cup from the floor and banged it on the bars. He kept it up for five minutes until a harried Sergeant Malbrough finally reappeared.

"Cut down on that racket!" he yelled. "You'll wake up my other two guests!"

"Sergeant, believe me. I'm a Secret Service agent. I'm a federal law enforcement man. Two notorious artists, Lambert G. Hanover and Teresa Salvare, are in New Orleans. I've been tracking them for two weeks now, after I was called to the case by my boss. They stole something like two-hundred thousand dollars in cash and negotiable stocks and bonds in a protracted Kansas City spree. The—"

Malbrough planted his hands on his hips and laughed. "Do tell?"

"I'm trying to!" Spur said, but he soon quenched his anger. "I'm no common criminal and I never tried to rape that woman. Look, Malbrough. What would it hurt to send a telegram to Washington? What would it hurt to wire General Halleck at the

Secret Service?"

The sergeant scratched his chin. "It'd cut into my leisure time. Oh, I'll admit you're a very smooth talker. But you're up against a very serious charge, Yankee. We don't cotton to men who try to take women against their will. Shit, McCoy, there's plenty of them who'll do it. They're all over the place—and not just the ones who charge, neither. My boy, you're in a heap of trouble."

Spur nodded. "Granted. Granted! Just send the telegram."

"Why should I go out of my way to waste my time on the likes of you?" he asked, and spat on the floor.

"Here." Spur dug into his pocket until he found what he'd been looking for. "Catch!"

Sergeant Malbrough's hand came down around the twenty-dollar gold piece that Spur flipped to him.

"The telegram's on me," McCoy said. "Okay?"

The Southern policeman whistled. "That's a lot of money. You tryin' to bribe me, boy?"

"Just send the damn telegram!" Spur said. "And, if it isn't too much trouble, have one of your men go to my room at the Hollister Hotel. Room twenty-five. If my bag hasn't been stolen, he'll find a document hidden inside the bottom explaining who I am and what my ongoing mission is."

Malbrough raised his eyebrows, took off his hat, wiped his forehead and grunted.

"Washington won't be too happy to hear that you've locked up one of their special law enforcement agents. It's best that you release me as soon as possible. These things do happen," Spur admitted, "but how'd you feel if I mistook you for a murderer, threw you into a cell and had the gallows readied to snap your neck before I even found out who you were? Think about that, Malbrough!"

The sergeant rubbed the gleaming coin. "Yeah. Well, I should send a wire to my cousin in New York anyway." He nodded. "Okay, McCoy. I'll do it, since you paid me. But just don't go anywhere." Malbrough laughed. "You hear me? Stay put?" He walked out.

Spur sat on the rickety bed and shook his head. A few minutes before he'd been thinking that this was the most confounding case he'd ever been on. Now, incredibly, it had gotten that much worse.

General Halleck will clear things up. Spur knew he would. But how soon? If he didn't get out by four, he only hoped that the *Natchez* would be late in leaving the wharf and sailing for St. Louis. That wasn't too likely since it was involved in the biggest race the Mississippi had ever known.

Teresa slipped into the Rue Orleans Hotel and quickly went to her room. Once inside she closed and locked the door and started undressing as she stared triumphantly at her finely dressed partner.

"How'd it go?" Lambert G. Hanover asked as he puffed on his cigar.

"Like a charm. Spur invited me into his room even. He knew who I was, all right, but he played along like he didn't. Finally, he called me by my real name, so I yelled rape like we'd planned." Teresa smiled. "The sergeant was very understanding as he interviewed me afterwards. Hell, I soaked his shoulder with my tears!"

"And? And?" Hanover stood. "What happened?"

"My dear Lamb, Spur McCoy—our enemy—is

locked up. Behind bars. The poor dear can't possibly stop us from boarding the steamer!"

Hanover blew out his breath. "Good. That settles that. Within hours we'll be mixing with the elegant crowd. We'll do everything that we've planned to do. Get to know the merchants, the planters, the foreign dignitaries. I'll gamble. You'll gossip and make new friends. Then, just before we dock at St. Louis, we'll go through as many of their staterooms as possible. We'll pick pockets like mad. We'll be among the first ones off. After that, it's the train and we'll be heading for San Francisco."

Teresa Salvare slipped the dress from her shoulders and stood in her chemise and petticoats. "Won't that be a glorious day, Lamb! No more running. No more hiding. I'm so tired of all this!"

"So am I." Hanover crushed out his cigar. "You sure are beautiful, Tessa, standing there in your underthings, your round, firm tits jutting against your chemise." He grinned and went to her.

"Why Lambert G. Hanover!" she said, throwing her hands over her bosom. "I'm shocked at such an ungentlemanlike statement coming from your lips."

"That's not all that's going to come from me."

He grabbed her. Teresa laughed as the man gently pulled her to the floor.

Spur stood motionless in his cell. One of the drunks coughed and rolled over on his bunk. There were no windows and no clocks in sight, but he knew he'd been locked up for at least two hours. If it got any later . . . .

The sound of the boots approaching the rear of the jail cell announced the return of Sergeant Malbrough. Sure enough, he soon appeared in the doorway holding a piece of paper.

"I'll be damned! I can't believe it!"

"Believe what?" Spur asked.

"Well, I sent the telegram like you asked me and waited around for an answer. You could've blown me over when the answer came back an hour or two later." The policeman shrugged. "I guess you are who you say you are. I wired this here Halleck fella what happened along with a description of you. He told me to let you go, that I was 'obstructing justice.' So I had one of my boys go to your hotel room. Sure enough, we found this."

Malbrough pushed a familiar piece of paper through the bars. Signed by General Halleck, it was a concise declaration that McCoy did indeed work for the United States Government. It didn't mention the Secret Service but it had apparently convinced the sergeant of his innocence.

"Sorry, McCoy. I guess that wild woman really is a thief." He grabbed the keys.

"She sure as shit is. I don't blame you, Malbrough. Just don't let it happen again."

"I won't." The man unlocked the cell. "You can count on that!"

"Where's my piece?" McCoy asked as he finally walked from the iron-barred prison.

"Right here." The sergeant pulled Spur's Colt .45 revolver from where he'd stashed it under the waist of his pants. "If I can help you out, let me know."

"You can start by telling me the time." Spur checked the cylinders and holstered his weapon.

"Time? Uh, think it's about 3:30. Something like that. Why? You going somewhere?"

Spur slapped a hand onto the crown of his hat and dashed for the door. "Yeah, I have a boat to catch!"·

CHAPTER EIGHTEEN

Spur McCoy bolted from the jail and shot into the street. It took him a second to get his bearings but he was soon off toward the distant wharves.

As he hurried through the streets of New Orleans, he had no idea if Sergeant Malbrough's guess at the time was correct. Two- and three-story buildings blocked a clear view of the two boats he was after. After a few minutes every street looked the same, the same hotels, the same wrought iron balconies, the same baskets filled with flowering plants.

McCoy slowed to let a buggy through the intersection and then took off again. His unfamiliarity with the city wasn't helping now that he had a deadline. Spur silently cursed Teresa Salvare until he finally got his bearings and headed straight for the wharves.

New steamboats had taken the places of the ones that had left since he'd been down by the river that morning. Spur smiled as he saw that both the *Robert*

E. Lee and the *Natchez* were both still in port.

Hundreds of people milled around before the grand steamers. It must be the wealthiest crowd ever assembled in New Orleans for any purpose. Between the gawkers and the men exchanging fistfuls of money for bets on the race's outcome, vendors hawked their wares and children cried. Spur saw at least two pickpockets at work but didn't give them any attention. He had bigger fish to catch.

He pushed his way through the people, patiently at first, excusing himself and tipping his hat to the ladies whom he squeezed by. Soon the crowd pressed toward the steamships, crushing him between a fetid fat man and an elderly woman barely able to hold herself up with her cane.

Then the shouting began. Shouts of jubilation, boasts of superior betting skill, challenges and counterchallenges between the opposing sides.

Applause broke out. Spur looked up to see the white-bearded captain of the *Robert E. Lee* walk up the gangplank to his steamboat. Though he couldn't be unaware of the crowd's presence he never acknowledged them, simply went onto his craft.

"The *Lee*'s taking off four minutes before the *Natchez,*" someone nearby yelled. "They'll make it into St. Louis before the Nuthatch slips its moors!"

"Oh yeah? Look, Knepher, I've told you again and again that leaving early don't mean they'll win. They'll have to take four minutes off their arrival time."

Passengers began boarding the *Natchez*. Spur felt his pulse quicken as he watched the procession of well-dressed women and men strolling onto the glistening steamer. He kept a close watch but didn't see anyone who resembled Hanover and Teresa. Still, they may already be on board.

Or they could be lost in the crowd. Spur angrily pushed through the people. As he tried to slip through the crowd, a large man banged him with his shoulders and knocked McCoy sideways. Only the sea of humanity kept him from tumbling from the ground.

Wisps of steam rose from the double lower stacks of both paddleboats. Sparks and thick black smoke belched out of the fluted tops of the larger chimneys, the remains of the firewood that the steamers were burning to heat its boilers. They were preparing to set sail.

He had to reach the *Natchez*.

The pockets hidden in Teresa Salvare's dress were bulging with the money she stolen from the crowd that had gathered to watch the start of the race. She was well pleased with the day's take but it was getting late.

The whistles from the *Natchez* warned her that it was time to find her partner and to board. But there were so many people and so little room that she bit her lower lip. Would she be able to meet him in time?

"All aboard!" a white-suited man called from the foot of the gangplank leading to the *Natchez*. "We leave in four minutes!"

Four men released her mooring lines and the *Robert E. Lee*, its stacks increasing their output by the second, nudged forward from the wharf. An American flag flapped proudly from her bow. The race was on.

Don't panic, Teresa told herself. You have four minutes. But what if she couldn't find Lamb? Should she get on without him?

No. He has the money. *He has the money!*

They'd agreed to meet by the gangplank just as the *Lee* left. Teresa realized that ladylike behavior wasn't called for here. She kicked and clawed her way through the crowd, getting through the people as fast as she could, forging her own trail through the human forest.

She made good progress, but her destination was still 50 feet away. Teresa bit her lip again. It hurt. She liked it.

"Miss Salvare!" a familiar voice called.

Teresa turned. Sergeant Malbrough waved his hat at her from several yards away. If the man knew her real name the game was over. She hurried twice as fast toward the safety of the steamboat.

"Come back here! You got me into a lot of trouble!" he yelled, as Teresa tried to melt into the crowd.

Spur kept an eye on the boarding passengers. No tall couple. No one who even remotely looked like them—so far. Unless he'd missed a face or two while dodging hundreds of sweating bodies.

He finally edged his way closer to the gangplank, nearly punched out a man to get past him and finally stood beside the uniformed officer.

"Good afternoon, sir," he said to Spur, beaming. "Get on board, please. We're about to embark. We have to maintain our schedule."

Spur waved him off and studied the men, women and the few children who stepped onto the *Natchez*. Behind him, the *Robert E. Lee* had pulled well into the water and was laboriously puffing its way up the Mississippi.

Half the crowd ran along the enbankment,

following the paddlewheel, while the *Natchez* supporters stayed put. The sudden thinning of the crowd gave Spur a better look at them. One face instantly stood out.

True, he'd shaved off his Van Dyke beard and lightly reddened his hair, but that was the man who'd knocked him out in Wet Prong. Spur was certain of it.

He was even more sure as the finely dressed man looked his way, recognized him and ran.

Spur dashed past three nuns and tackled the tall thief. Hanover dropped the two leather bags he'd been carrying and went down on the ground. Spur sat on his chest and slammed his fist into the man's jaw. His well-placed punches soon did their damage. The skin broke. Blood appeared beneath his knuckles.

"Lamb!" a woman's voice called.

"Miss Salvare!"

"Someone help that poor man!"

He punched Hanover twice more until the groggy man's head fell back. He was out cold.

Spur shot to his feet. Three yards behind him, Teresa Salvare stood frozen, her hands limp at her sides, her mouth open.

"Come here. The game's over," McCoy said, panting.

Teresa turned to run but stopped as she saw Sergeant Malbrough approaching her with his revolver out and ready for business. The woman screamed and bolted for the gangplank, which a pair of roustabouts were just removing from the *Natchez*.

"No. Wait!" she wailed.

Spur easily cut her off and caught the beautiful

woman in his arms. "Don't fight it," he said.
"Malbrough!" he shouted as Teresa dissolved into
tears.

"Yes sir!" came the prompt response.

"Get those two bags! Beside Hanover!"

"Already got them, McCoy."

Spur smiled down at Teresa. "You can stop
acting," he said. "I'm not buying it."

"Good. Because I'm not selling it."

Malbrough appeared with the leather bags in one
hand. In the other he held Hanover's belt and the
back of his pants. He'd dragged the man there.

"Let's lock these two up. I've been this close to
them so often that I don't doubt they'd try to slip
away again. And remember, Malbrough, we have to
deliver them alive!"

The police sergeant clicked together his heels.
"Yes sir!"

"Bastard!" Teresa Salvare said. "You bastard!
We could have gotten away with it!" She spat.

Spur smiled as the warm saliva ran down his
cheek. "But you got cold feet. Why didn't you kill
me yesterday morning in your room? You had the
chance."

She turned her head.

McCoy pulled her closer. "Come on. Why didn't
you?"

"I—" The lovely criminal faced him again. Tears
splashed her face. "Because you were so goddamn
handsome that I lost my mind."

He laughed. "Okay, Malbrough. Let's get this
trash off the wharf."

"My feelings exactly, McCoy."

Spur released one of Teresa's arms. "Hand me the
bags. You take Hanover."

The woman stamped McCoy's foot with her boot. He howled. At the height of his unexpected pain she wriggled out of his grasp and ran.

"Damn it, woman!" Spur shouted. He took two flying paces and grabbed her waist, halting the woman's flight. "Not again. Not this time, Teresa."

"Let me go! Leave me alone!" she screamed.

He took her back to where Sergeant Malbrough still stood, holding out the bags for Spur.

"You're absolutely sure these are the ones?" the policeman said.

"Here. Take this." He pushed Teresa into the man's arms and took the bags. They were well packed. Inside he didn't find any clothes. No petticoats or handkerchiefs or fancy dresses made the sides bulge.

Spur McCoy pulled out a wad of cash.

"Yes," he said.

CHAPTER NINETEEN

At seven that evening, Spur McCoy was in his hotel room packing his bags. He'd just been to see Sergeant Malbrough again to assure himself that Lambert G. Hanover and Teresa Salvare were still behind bars.

Fortunately, they were, and Malbrough said that while the man wasn't saying a word, the woman was spilling out all the details of their "work." She almost seemed proud of it, the policeman had told him.

Spur had suggested that Malbrough put on extra guards and he had instantly done so.

Now, as he bent over his leather bags, Spur sighed. His work in New Orleans was nearly finished. All he had to do was transport the pair back to Kansas City.

That wouldn't be an easy task, not with them. Hanover and Teresa were experts at slipping away from him, so Spur had decided to take precautions to make sure that he managed to get them safely back to the city where they'd started their more recent crimes.

Travelling by buggy or horseback was out. It was too unpredictable and unsafe, not to mention the distance and travel time involved. Spur had searched for another way and was glad to hear that the steamboat *City of Charles* was leaving for Kansas City in two days. He booked passage.

Sure, it might be humiliating for Teresa and Lambert to spend five or six days in chains, but it was the only way he could be certain that they wouldn't escape. Sergeant Malbrough had offered to send a policeman along with Spur to keep an eye on the couple. It was a good idea and he had readily agreed to bring the fresh-faced young man with them.

He'd gone through the single bag that the pair had planned to take with them (the others, he thought, had probably been loaded on board, but there was no stopping the *Natchez* during its cruise to history). He'd counted precisely $110,000 in both bills and gold coins. Apparently even fussy when it came to money, Hanover had either only taken $100 bills or he'd had it changed into the higher denominations along the way. The money was clean and neatly stacked.

There were hundreds of stocks and negotiable bonds as well. It didn't look like they'd spent too much on their two and a half week trip from Kansas City to New Orleans.

Spur had wired General Halleck his final report on the case. He could relax for the next day. There were no immediate problems, no criminals to capture.

He poured himself a drink, sipped the bitter liquid and put down his glass. He knew what he wanted, and he couldn't find it at the bottom of a whiskey bottle.

Spur changed into his best clothes and left his hotel room. The Gilded Garter Gambling Establishment beckoned to him, but he passed it by. The prostitutes called to him but he wasn't interested in them.

He was hungry.

What was the name of the restaurant? The one that Sergeant Malbrough had suggested to him? Spur searched the eating establishments. Finally he saw a familiar name on one of their signs: Pierre's.

He moved across the street and walked in. The air smelled of sizzling steaks and grilled seafood. Elegantly dressed men and women laughed, ate and danced to the music of a four-piece string quartet. Spur stood just inside.

"McCoy!" a voice yelled.

Spur turned and saw the burly policeman.

"Come on over here!" The cop said, broadly smiling as he sat at a table with his arms around two women. Both were dripping with jewels.

McCoy smiled and went to them. The girls smelled of perfume. Their gowns were lavish. They were strikingly beautiful and, from the way they resembled each other, probably sisters. Both had masses of raven hair and green eyes.

"Hello, sergeant," Spur said.

Malbrough cleared his throat. "Hi yerself. Found the place alright, I see."

"No problem."

"Spur McCoy, I'd like you to meet Violette and Helena Rosengarten. They're sisters. Can't you tell?

Just got in from Prussia. Isn't that right?"

"*Guten tag,*" they both said, then exploded into high pitched laughter.

The sergeant leaned over the table toward him. "They don't speak a word of English, but that's no problem. They speak everything else." He settled back in his velvet-cushioned chair and squeezed Helena's shoulder. "Isn't that right, doll?"

"Ladies," Spur said in greeting, touching the brim of his hat.

The younger of the two, Violette, fixed her gaze on Spur's face and played with the pearls that hung around her neck.

"So sit down!" Malbrough yelled. "Take a load off your feet and order a drink on me. We're just about to catch a bite to eat."

"Great. I'm starving."

Violette stared at him. She raised her glass and touched her tongue to its rim. Never taking her eyes off him, the beautiful woman licked back and forth.

Spur smiled and she returned the feeling. He knew—or hoped he knew—what would happen after dinner with the vivacious foreign woman.

But in two days he'd be back at work. Once he'd dropped off Teresa and Hanover in Kansas City, General Halleck would be sending him another assignment. It was times like this, between jobs, that he felt it was all worthwhile.

He sighed as Violette placed her glass on the table and boldly took his hand in hers. It sure was good to be back among the living again.